Lost Illusions
Volume I

Honore de Balzac

Copyright Notice

The text in this book has been downloaded from the internet and has been extensively edited and typeset.

CONTENTS

Introduction

The longest, without exception, of Balzac's books, and one which contains hardly any passage that is not very nearly of his best, *Illusions Perdues* suffers, I think, a little in point of composition from the mixture of the Angouleme scenes of its first and third parts with the purely Parisian interest of *Un Grand Homme de Province*. It is hardly possible to exaggerate the gain in distinctness and lucidity of arrangement derived from putting *Les Deux Poetes* and *Eve et David1* together in one volume, and reserving the greatness and decadence of Lucien de Rubempre for another. It is distinctly awkward that this should be divided, as it is itself an enormous episode, a sort of Herodotean parenthesis, rather than an integral part of the story. And, as a matter of fact, it joins on much more to the *Splendeurs et Miseres des Courtisanes* than to its actual companions. In fact, it is an instance of the somewhat haphazard and arbitrary way in which the actual division of the *Comedie* has worked, that it should, dealing as it does wholly and solely with Parisian life, be put in the *Scenes de la Vie de Province*, and should be separated from its natural conclusion not merely as a matter of volumes, but as a matter of divisions. In making the arrangement, however, it is necessary to remember Balzac's own scheme, especially as the connection of the three parts in other ways is too close to permit the wrenching of them asunder altogether and finally. This caution given, all that is necessary can be done by devoting the first part of the introduction entirely to the first and third or Angouleme parts, and by consecrating the latter part to the egregious Lucien by himself.

There is a double gain in doing this, for, independently of the connection as above referred to, Lucien has little to do except as an opportunity for the display of virtue by his sister and David Sechard; and the parts in which they appear are among the most interesting of Balzac's work. The "Idyllic" charm of this marriage for love, combined as it is with exhibitions of the author's power in more than one of the ways in which he loved best to show it, has never escaped attention from Balzac's most competent critics. He himself had speculated in print and paper before David Sechard was conceived; he himself had for all "maniacs," all men of one idea, the fraternal enthusiasm of a fellow-victim. He could never touch a miser without a sort of shudder of interest; and that singular fancy of his for describing complicated legal and commercial undertakings came in too. Nor did he spare, in this wide-ranging book, to bring in other favorite matters of his, the *hobereau* – or squireen – aristocracy, the tittle-tattle of the country town and so forth.

The result is a book of multifarious interest, not hampered, as some of its fellows are, by an uncertainty on the author's part as to what particular hare he is coursing. Part of the interest, after the description of the printing office and of old Sechard's swindling of his son, is a doubling, it is true, upon that of *La muse du Departement*, and is perhaps a little less amusingly done; but it is blended with better matters. Sixte du Chatelet is a considerable addition to Balzac's gallery of the aristocracy in transition – of the Bonaparte *parvenus* whom perhaps he understood even better than the old nobility, for they were already in his time becoming adulterated and alloyed; or than the new folk of business and finance, for they were but in their earliest stages. Nor is the rest of the society of Madame de Bargeton inferior.

But the real interest both of *Les Deux Poetes*, and still more of *Eve et David*, between which two, be it always remembered, comes in the *Distinguished Provincial*, lies in the characters who gave their name to the last part. In David, the man of one idea, who yet has room for an honest love and an all-deserved friendship, Balzac could not go wrong. David Sechard takes a place by himself among the sheep of the *Comedie*. Some may indeed say that this phrase is unfortunate, that Balzac's sheep have more qualities of the mutton than innocence. It is not quite to be denied. But David is very far indeed from being a good imbecile, like Cesar Birotteau, or a man intoxicated out of common-sense by a passion respectable in itself, like Goriot. His sacrifice of his mania in time is something – nay,

IV

it is very much; and his disinterested devotion to his brother-in-law does not quite pass the limits of sense.

But what shall we say of Eve? She is good of course, good as gold, as Eugenie Grandet herself; and the novelist has been kind enough to allow her to be happier. But has he quite interested us in her love for David? Has he even persuaded us that the love existed in a form deserving the name? Did not Eve rather take her husband to protect him, to look after him, than either to love, honor, and obey in the orthodox sense, or to love for love's sake only, as some still take their husbands and wives even at the end of the nineteenth century? This is a question which each reader must answer for himself; but few are likely to refuse assent to the sentence, "Happy the husband who has such a wife as Eve Chardon!"

The central part of *Illusions Perdues*, which in reason stands by itself, and may do so ostensibly with considerably less than the introduction explanatory which Balzac often gives to his own books, is one of the most carefully worked out and diversely important of his novels. It should, of course, be read before *Splendeurs et Miseres des Courtisanes*, which is avowedly its second part, a small piece of *Eve et David* serving as the link between them. But it is almost sufficient by and to itself. *Lucien de Rubempre ou le Journalisme* would be the most straightforward and descriptive title for it, and one which Balzac in some of his moods would have been content enough to use.

The story of it is too continuous and interesting to need elaborate argument, for nobody is likely to miss any important link in it. But Balzac has nowhere excelled in finesse and success of analysis, the double disillusion which introduces itself at once between Madame de Bargeton and Lucien, and which makes any *redintegratio amoris* of a valid kind impossible, because each cannot but be aware that the other has anticipated the rupture. It will not, perhaps, be a matter of such general agreement whether he has or has not exceeded the fair license of the novelist in attributing to Lucien those charms of body and gifts of mind which make him, till his moral weakness and worthlessness are exposed, irresistible, and enable him for a time to repair his faults by a sort of fairy good-luck. The sonnets of *Les Marguerites*, which were given to the author by poetical friends – Gautier, it is said, supplied the "Tulip" – are undoubtedly good and sufficient. But Lucien's first article, which is (according to a practice the rashness of which cannot be too much deprecated) given likewise, is certainly not very wonderful; and the Paris press must have been rather at a low ebb if it made any sensation. As we are not favored with any actual portrait of Lucien, detection is less possible here, but the novelist has perhaps a very little abused the privilege of making a hero,

"Like Paris handsome, and like Hector brave," or rather "Like Paris handsome, and like Phoebus clever." There is no doubt, however, that the interest of the book lies partly in the vivid and severe picture of journalism given in it, and partly in the way in which the character of Lucien is adjusted to show up that of the abstract journalist still farther.

How far is the picture true? It must be said, in fairness to Balzac, that a good many persons of some competence in France have pronounced for its truth there; and if that be so, all one can say is, "So much the worse for French journalists." It is also certain that a lesser, but still not inconsiderable number of persons in England – generally persons who, not perhaps with Balzac's genius, have like Balzac published books, and are not satisfied with their reception by the press – agree more or less as to England. For myself, I can only say that I do not believe things have ever been quite so bad in England, and that I am quite sure there never has been any need for them to be. There are, no doubt, spiteful, unprincipled, incompetent practitioners of journalism as of everything else; and it is of course obvious that while advertisements, the favor of the chiefs of parties, and so forth, are temptations to newspaper managers not to hold up a very high standard of honor, anonymity affords to newspaper writers a dangerously easy shield to cover malice or dishonesty. But I can only say that during long practice in every kind of political and literary journalism, I never was seriously asked to write anything I did not think, and never had the slightest difficulty in confining myself to what I did think.

In fact Balzac, like a good many other men of letters who abuse journalism, put himself very much out of court by continually practising it, not merely during his struggling period, but long after he had made his name, indeed almost to the very last. And it is very hard to resist the conclusion that when he charged journalism generally not merely with envy, hatred, malice, and all uncharitableness, but with hopeless and pervading dishonesty, he had little more ground for it than an inability to conceive how any one, except from vile reasons of this kind, could fail to praise Honore de Balzac.

At any rate, either his art by itself, or his art assisted and strengthened by that personal feeling which, as we have seen counted for much with him, has here produced a wonderfully vivid piece of fiction – one, I think, inferior in success to hardly anything he has done. Whether, as at a late period a very well-informed, well-affected, and well-equipped critic hinted, his picture of the Luciens and the Lousteaus did not a little to propagate both is another matter. The seriousness with which Balzac took the accusation perhaps shows a little sense of galling. But putting this aside, *Un Grand Homme de Province a Paris* must be ranked, both for comedy and tragedy, both for scheme and execution, in the first rank of his work.

The bibliography of this long and curious book – almost the only one which contains some verse, some of Balzac's own, some given to him by his more poetical friends – occupies full ten pages of M. de Lovenjoul's record. The first part, which bore the general title, was a book from the beginning, and appeared in 1837 in the *Scenes de la Vie de Province*. It had five chapters, and the original verse it contained had appeared in the *Annalaes Romantiques* ten years earlier with slight variants. The second part, *Un Grand Homme de Province*, likewise appeared as a book, independently published by Souverain in 1839 in two volumes and forty chapters. But two of these chapters had been inserted a few days before the publications in the *Estafette*. Here Canalis was more distinctly identified with Lamartine than in the subsequent texts. The third part, unlike its forerunners, appeared serially in two papers, *L'Etat* and *Le Parisien*, in the year 1843, under the title of *David Sechard, ou les Souffrances d'un Inventeur*, and next year became a book under the first title only. But before this last issue it had been united to the other two parts, and had appeared as *Eve et David* in the first edition of the *Comedie*.

George Saintsbury

Dedication

To Monsieur Victor Hugo,

It was your birthright to be, like a Rafael or a Pitt, a great poet at an age when other men are children; it was your fate, the fate of Chateaubriand and of every man of genius, to struggle against jealousy skulking behind the columns of a newspaper, or crouching in the subterranean places of journalism. For this reason I desired that your victorious name should help to win a victory for this work that I inscribe to you, a work which, if some persons are to be believed, is an act of courage as well as a veracious history. If there had been journalists in the time of Moliere, who can doubt but that they, like marquises, financiers, doctors, and lawyers, would have been within the province of the writer of plays? And why should Comedy, *qui castigat ridendo mores*, make an exception in favor of one power, when the Parisian press spares none? I am happy, monsieur, in this opportunity of subscribing myself your sincere admirer and friend,

DE BALZAC.

TWO POETS

At the time when this story opens, the Stanhope press and the ink-distributing roller were not as yet in general use in small provincial printing establishments. Even at Angouleme, so closely connected through its paper-mills with the art of typography in Paris, the only machinery in use was the primitive wooden invention to which the language owes a figure of speech – "the press groans" was no mere rhetorical expression in those days. Leather ink-balls were still used in old-fashioned printing houses; the pressman dabbed the ink by hand on the characters, and the movable table on which the form of type was placed in readiness for the sheet of paper, being made of marble, literally deserved its name of "impression-stone." Modern machinery has swept all this old-world mechanism into oblivion; the wooden press which, with all its imperfections, turned out such beautiful work for the Elzevirs, Plantin, Aldus, and Didot is so completely forgotten, that something must be said as to the obsolete gear on which Jerome-Nicolas Sechard set an almost superstitious affection, for it plays a part in this chronicle of great small things.

Sechard had been in his time a journeyman pressman, a "bear" in compositors' slang. The continued pacing to and fro of the pressman from ink-table to press, from press to ink-table, no doubt suggested the nickname. The "bears," however, make matters even by calling the compositors monkeys, on account of the nimble industry displayed by those gentlemen in picking out the type from the hundred and fifty-two compartments of the cases.

In the disastrous year 1793, Sechard, being fifty years old and a married man, escaped the great Requisition which swept the bulk of French workmen into the army. The old pressman was the only hand left in the printing-house; and when the master (otherwise the "gaffer) died, leaving a widow, but no children, the business seemed to be on the verge of extinction; for the solitary "bear" was quite incapable of the feat of transformation into a "monkey," and in his quality of pressman had never learned to read or write. Just then, however, a Representative of the People being in a mighty hurry to publish the Decrees of the Convention, bestowed a master printer's license on Sechard, and requisitioned the establishment. Citizen Sechard accepted the dangerous patent, bought the business of his master's widow with his wife's savings, and took over the plant at half its value. But he was not even at the beginning. He was bound to print the Decrees of the Republic without mistakes and without delay.

In this strait Jerome-Nicolas Sechard had the luck to discover a noble Marseillais who had no mind to emigrate and lose his lands, nor yet to show himself openly and lose his head, and consequently was fain to earn a living by some lawful industry. A bargain was struck. M. le Comte de Maucombe, disguised in a provincial printer's jacket, set up, read, and corrected the decrees which forbade citizens to harbor aristocrats under pain of death; while the "bear," now a "gaffer," printed the copies and duly posted them, and the pair remained safe and sound.

In 1795, when the squall of the Terror had passed over, Nicolas Sechard was obliged to look out for another jack-of-all-trades to be compositor, reader, and foreman in one; and an Abbe who declined the oath succeeded the Comte de Maucombe as soon as the First Consul restored public worship. The Abbe became a Bishop at the Restoration, and in after days the Count and the Abbe met and sat together on the same bench of the House of Peers.

In 1795 Jerome-Nicolas had not known how to read or write; in 1802 he had made no progress in either art; but by allowing a handsome margin for "wear and tear" in his estimates, he managed to pay a foreman's wages. The once easy-going journeyman was a terror to his "bears" and "monkeys." Where poverty ceases, avarice begins. From the day when Sechard first caught a glimpse of the possibility of making a fortune, a growing covetousness developed and sharpened in him a certain practical faculty for business –

greedy, suspicious, and keen-eyed. He carried on his craft in disdain of theory. In course of time he had learned to estimate at a glance the cost of printing per page or per sheet in every kind of type. He proved to unlettered customers that large type costs more to move; or, if small type was under discussion, that it was more difficult to handle. The setting-up of the type was the one part of his craft of which he knew nothing; and so great was his terror lest he should not charge enough, that he always made a heavy profit. He never took his eyes off his compositors while they were paid by the hour. If he knew that a paper manufacturer was in difficulties, he would buy up his stock at a cheap rate and warehouse the paper. So from this time forward he was his own landlord, and owned the old house which had been a printing office from time immemorial.

He had every sort of luck. He was left a widower with but one son. The boy he sent to the grammar school; he must be educated, not so much for his own sake as to train a successor to the business; and Sechard treated the lad harshly so as to prolong the time of parental rule, making him work at case on holidays, telling him that he must learn to earn his own living, so as to recompense his poor old father, who was slaving his life out to give him an education.

Then the Abbe went, and Sechard promoted one of his four compositors to be foreman, making his choice on the future bishop's recommendation of the man as an honest and intelligent workman. In these ways the worthy printer thought to tide over the time until his son could take a business which was sure to extend in young and clever hands.

David Sechard's school career was a brilliant one. Old Sechard, as a "bear" who had succeeded in life without any education, entertained a very considerable contempt for attainments in book learning; and when he sent his son to Paris to study the higher branches of typography, he recommended the lad so earnestly to save a good round sum in the "working man's paradise" (as he was pleased to call the city), and so distinctly gave the boy to understand that he was not to draw upon the paternal purse, that it seemed as if old Sechard saw some way of gaining private ends of his own by that sojourn in the Land of Sapience. So David learned his trade, and completed his education at the same time, and Didot's foreman became a scholar; and yet when he left Paris at the end of 1819, summoned home by his father to take the helm of business, he had not cost his parent a farthing.

Now Nicolas Sechard's establishment hitherto had enjoyed a monopoly of all the official printing in the department, besides the work of the prefecture and the diocese – three connections which should prove mighty profitable to an active young printer; but precisely at this juncture the firm of Cointet Brothers, paper manufacturers, applied to the authorities for the second printer's license in Angouleme. Hitherto old Sechard had contrived to reduce this license to a dead letter, thanks to the war crisis of the Empire, and consequent atrophy of commercial enterprise; but he had neglected to buy up the right himself, and this piece of parsimony was the ruin of the old business. Sechard thought joyfully when he heard the news that the coming struggle with the Cointets would be fought out by his son and not by himself.

"I should have gone to the wall," he thought, "but a young fellow from the Didots will pull through."

The septuagenarian sighed for the time when he could live at ease in his own fashion. If his knowledge of the higher branches of the craft of printing was scanty, on the other hand, he was supposed to be past master of an art which workmen pleasantly call "tipple-ography," an art held in high esteem by the divine author of *Pantagruel*; though of late, by reason of the persecution of societies yclept of Temperance, the cult has fallen, day by day, into disuse.

Jerome-Nicolas Sechard, bound by the laws of etymology to be a dry subject, suffered from an inextinguishable thirst. His wife, during her lifetime, managed to control within reasonable bounds the passion for the juice of the grape, a taste so natural to the bear that M. de Chateaubriand remarked it among the ursine tribes of the New World. But philosophers inform us that old age is apt to revert to the habits of youth, and Sechard senior is a case in point – the older he grew, the better he loved to drink. The master-passion had given a stamp of originality to an ursine physiognomy; his nose had developed till it reached the proportions of a double great-canon A; his veined cheeks looked like vine-leaves, covered, as they were, with bloated patches of purple, madder red, and often mottled hues; till altogether, the countenance suggested a huge truffle clasped about by autumn vine tendrils. The little gray eyes, peering out from beneath thick eyebrows like bushes covered with snow, were agleam with the cunning of avarice that had extinguished everything else in the man, down to the very instinct of fatherhood. Those eyes never lost their cunning even when disguised in drink. Sechard put you in mind of one of La Fontaine's Franciscan friars, with the fringe of grizzled hair still curling about his bald pate. He was short and corpulent, like one of the old-fashioned lamps for illumination, that burn a vast deal of oil to a very small piece of wick; for excess of any sort confirms the habit of body, and drunkenness, like much study, makes the fat man stouter, and the lean man leaner still.

For thirty years Jerome-Nicolas-Sechard had worn the famous municipal three-cornered hat, which you may still see here and there on the head of the towncrier in out-of-the-way places. His breeches and waistcoat were of greenish velveteen, and he wore an old-fashioned brown greatcoat, gray cotton stockings, and shoes with silver buckles to them. This costume, in which the workman shone through the burgess, was so thoroughly in keeping with the man's character, defects, and way of life, that he might have come ready dressed into the world. You could no more imagine him apart from his clothes than you could think of a bulb without its husk. If the old printer had not long since given the measure of his blind greed, the very nature of the man came out in the manner of his abdication.

Knowing, as he did, that his son must have learned his business pretty thoroughly in the great school of the Didots, he had yet been ruminating for a long while over the bargain that he meant to drive with David. All that the father made, the son, of course, was bound to lose, but in business this worthy knew nothing of father or son. If, in the first instance, he had looked on David as his only child, later he came to regard him as the natural purchaser of the business, whose interests were therefore his own. Sechard meant to sell dear; David, of course, to buy cheap; his son, therefore, was an antagonist, and it was his duty to get the better of him. The transformation of sentiment into self-seeking, ordinarily slow, tortuous, and veiled by hypocrisy in better educated people, was swift and direct in the old "bear," who demonstrated the superiority of shrewd tipple-ography over book-learned typography.

David came home, and the old man received him with all the cordiality which cunning folk can assume with an eye to business. He was as full of thought for him as any lover for his mistress; giving him his arm, telling him where to put his foot down so as to avoid the mud, warming the bed for him, lighting a fire in his room, making his supper ready. The next day, after he had done his best to fluster his son's wits over a sumptuous dinner, Jerome-Nicolas Sechard, after copious potations, began with a "Now for business," a remark so singularly misplaced between two hiccoughs, that David begged his parent to postpone serious matters until the morrow. But the old "bear" was by no means inclined to put off the long-expected battle; he was too well prepared to turn his tipsiness to good account. He had dragged the chain these fifty years, he would not wear it another hour; to-morrow his son should be the "gaffer."

Perhaps a word or two about the business premises may be said here. The printing-house had been established since the reign of Louis XIV. in the angle made by the Rue de Beaulieu and the Place du Murier; it had been devoted to its present purposes for a long time past. The ground floor consisted of a single huge room lighted on the side next the street by an old-fashioned casement, and by a large sash window that gave upon the yard at the back. A passage at the side led to the private office; but in the provinces the processes of typography excite such a lively interest, that customers usually preferred to enter by way of the glass door in the street front, though they at once descended three steps, for the floor of the workshop lay below the level of the street. The gaping newcomer always failed to note the perils of the passage through the shop; and while staring at the sheets of paper strung in groves across the ceiling, ran against the rows of cases, or knocked his hat against the tie-bars that secured the presses in position. Or the customer's eyes would follow the agile movements of a compositor, picking out type from the hundred and fifty-two compartments of his case, reading his copy, verifying the words in the composing-stick, and leading the lines, till a ream of damp paper weighted with heavy slabs, and set down in the middle of the gangway, tripped up the bemused spectator, or he caught his hip against the angle of a bench, to the huge delight of boys, "bears," and "monkeys." No wight had ever been known to reach the further end without accident. A couple of glass-windowed cages had been built out into the yard at the back; the foreman sat in state in the one, the master printer in the other. Out in the yard the walls were agreeably decorated by trellised vines, a tempting bit of color, considering the owner's reputation. On the one side of the space stood the kitchen, on the other the woodshed, and in a ramshackle penthouse against the hall at the back, the paper was trimmed and damped down. Here, too, the forms, or, in ordinary language, the masses of set-up type, were washed. Inky streams issuing thence blended with the ooze from the kitchen sink, and found their way into the kennel in the street outside; till peasants coming into the town of a market day believed that the Devil was taking a wash inside the establishment.

As to the house above the printing office, it consisted of three rooms on the first floor and a couple of attics in the roof. The first room did duty as dining-room and lobby; it was exactly the same length as the passage below, less the space taken up by the old-fashioned wooden staircase; and was lighted by a narrow casement on the street and a bull's-eye window looking into the yard. The chief characteristic of the apartment was a cynic simplicity, due to money-making greed. The bare walls were covered with plain whitewash, the dirty brick floor had never been scoured, the furniture consisted of three rickety chairs, a round table, and a sideboard stationed between the two doors of a bedroom and a sitting-room. Windows and doors alike were dingy with accumulated grime. Reams of blank paper or printed matter usually encumbered the floor, and more frequently than not the remains of Sechard's dinner, empty bottles and plates, were lying about on the packages.

The bedroom was lighted on the side of the yard by a window with leaded panes, and hung with the old-world tapestry that decorated house fronts in provincial towns on Corpus Christi Day. For furniture it boasted a vast four-post bedstead with canopy, valances and quilt of crimson serge, a couple of worm-eaten armchairs, two tapestry-covered chairs in walnut wood, an aged bureau, and a timepiece on the mantel-shelf. The Seigneur Rouzeau, Jerome-Nicolas' master and predecessor, had furnished the homely old-world room; it was just as he had left it.

The sitting-room had been partly modernized by the late Mme. Sechard; the walls were adorned with a wainscot, fearful to behold, painted the color of powder blue. The panels were decorated with wall-paper – Oriental scenes in sepia tint – and for all furniture, half-a-dozen chairs with lyre-shaped backs and blue leather cushions were ranged round the room. The two clumsy arched windows that gave upon the Place du Murier were curtainless; there was neither clock nor candle sconce nor mirror above the mantel-shelf, for Mme. Sechard had died before she carried out her scheme of decoration; and the "bear," unable to conceive the use of improvements that brought in no return in money, had left it at this point.

Hither, *pede titubante*, Jerome-Nicolas Sechard brought his son, and pointed to a sheet of paper lying on the table – a valuation of plant drawn up by the foreman under his direction.

"Read that, my boy," said Jerome-Nicolas, rolling a drunken eye from the paper to his son, and back to the paper. "You will see what a jewel of a printing-house I am giving you."

"'Three wooden presses, held in position by iron tie-bars, cast-iron plates...'"

"An improvement of my own," put in Sechard senior.

"'...Together with all the implements, ink-tables, balls, benches, et cetera, sixteen hundred francs!' Why, father," cried David, letting the sheet fall, "these presses of yours are old sabots not worth a hundred crowns; they are only fit for firewood."

"Sabots?" cried old Sechard, "*Sabots*? There, take the inventory and let us go downstairs. You will soon see whether your paltry iron-work contrivances will work like these solid old tools, tried and trusty. You will not have the heart after that to slander honest old presses that go like mail coaches, and are good to last you your lifetime without needing repairs of any sort. Sabots! Yes, sabots that are like to hold salt enough to cook your eggs with – sabots that your father has plodded on with these twenty years; they have helped him to make you what you are."

The father, without coming to grief on the way, lurched down the worn, knotty staircase that shook under his tread. In the passage he opened the door of the workshop, flew to the nearest press (artfully oiled and cleaned for the occasion) and pointed out the strong oaken cheeks, polished up by the apprentice.

"Isn't it a love of a press?"

A wedding announcement lay in the press. The old "bear" folded down the frisket upon the tympan, and the tympan upon the form, ran in the carriage, worked the lever, drew out the carriage, and lifted the frisket and tympan, all with as much agility as the youngest of the tribe. The press, handled in this sort, creaked aloud in such fine style that you might have thought some bird had dashed itself against the window pane and flown away again.

"Where is the English press that could go at that pace?" the parent asked of his astonished son.

Old Sechard hurried to the second, and then to the third in order, repeating the manoeuvre with equal dexterity. The third presenting to his wine-troubled eye a patch overlooked by the apprentice, with a notable oath he rubbed it with the skirt of his overcoat, much as a horse-dealer polishes the coat of an animal that he is trying to sell.

"With those three presses, David, you can make your nine thousand francs a year without a foreman. As your future partner, I am opposed to your replacing these presses by your cursed cast-iron machinery, that wears out the type. You in Paris have been making such a to-do over that damned Englishman's invention – a foreigner, an enemy of France who wants to help the ironfounders to a fortune. Oh! you wanted Stanhopes, did you? Thanks for your Stanhopes, that cost two thousand five hundred francs apiece, about twice as much as my three jewels put together, and maul your type to pieces, because there is no give in them. I haven't book-learning like you, but you keep this well in mind, the life of the Stanhope is the death of the type. Those three presses will serve your turn well enough, the printing will be properly done, and folk here in Angouleme won't ask any more of you. You may print with presses made of wood or iron or gold or silver, *they* will never pay you a farthing more."

"'Item,'" pursued David, "'five thousand pounds weight of type from M. Vaflard's foundry...'" Didot's apprentice could not help smiling at the name.

"Laugh away! After twelve years of wear, that type is as good as new. That is what I call a typefounder! M. Vaflard is an honest man, who uses hard metal; and, to my way of thinking, the best typefounder is the one you go to most seldom."

"'...Taken at ten thousand francs,'" continued David. "Ten thousand francs, father! Why, that is two francs a pound, and the Messrs. Didot only ask thirty-six sous for their *Cicero*! These nail-heads of yours will only fetch the price of old metal – fivepence a pound."

"You call M. Gille's italics, running-hand and round-hand, 'nail-heads,' do you? M. Gille, that used to be printer to the Emperor! And type that costs six francs a pound! master-pieces of engraving, bought only five years ago. Some of them are as bright yet as when they came from the foundry. Look here!"

Old Sechard pounced upon some packets of unused sorts, and held them out for David to see.

"I am not book-learned; I don't know how to read or write; but, all the same, I know enough to see that M. Gille's sloping letters are the fathers of your Messrs. Didot's English running-hand. Here is the round-hand," he went on, taking up an unused pica type.

David saw that there was no way of coming to terms with his father. It was a case of Yes or No – of taking or leaving it. The very ropes across the ceiling had gone down into the old "bear's" inventory, and not the smallest item was omitted; jobbing chases, wetting-boards, paste-pots, rinsing-trough, and lye-brushes had all been put down and valued separately with miserly exactitude. The total amounted to thirty thousand francs, including the license and the goodwill. David asked himself whether or not this thing was feasible.

Old Sechard grew uneasy over his son's silence; he would rather have had stormy argument than a wordless acceptance of the situation. Chaffering in these sorts of bargains means that a man can look after his interests. "A man who is ready to pay you anything you ask will pay nothing," old Sechard was saying to himself. While he tried to follow his son's train of thought, he went through the list of odds and ends of plant needed by a country business, drawing David now to a hot-press, now to a cutting-press, bragging of its usefulness and sound condition.

"Old tools are always the best tools," said he. "In our line of business they ought to fetch more than the new, like goldbeaters' tools."

Hideous vignettes, representing Hymen and Cupids, skeletons raising the lids of their tombs to describe a V or an M, and huge borders of masks for theatrical posters became in turn objects of tremendous value through old Jerome-Nicolas' vinous eloquence. Old custom, he told his son, was so deeply rooted in the district that he (David) would only waste his pains if he gave them the finest things in life. He himself had tried to sell them a better class of almanac than the *Double Liegeois* on grocers' paper; and what came of it? – the original *Double Liegeois* sold better than the most sumptuous calendars. David would soon see the importance of these old-fashioned things when he found he could get more for them than for the most costly new-fangled articles.

"Aha! my boy, Paris is Paris, and the provinces are the provinces. If a man came in from L'Houmeau with an order for wedding cards, and you were to print them without a Cupid and garlands, he would not believe that he was properly married; you would have them all back again if you sent them out with a plain M on them after the style of your Messrs. Didot. They may be fine printers, but their inventions won't take in the provinces for another hundred years. So there you are."

A generous man is a bad bargain-driver. David's nature was of the sensitive and affectionate type that shrinks from a dispute, and gives way at once if an opponent touches his feelings. His loftiness of feeling, and the fact that the old toper had himself well in hand, put him still further at a disadvantage in a dispute about money matters with his own father, especially as he credited that father with the best intentions, and took his covetous greed for a printer's attachment to his old familiar tools. Still, as Jerome-Nicolas Sechard had taken the whole place over from Rouzeau's widow for ten thousand francs, paid in assignats, it stood to reason that thirty thousand francs in coin at the present day was an exorbitant demand.

"Father, you are cutting my throat!" exclaimed David.

"*I*," cried the old toper, raising his hand to the lines of cord across the ceiling, "I who gave you life? Why, David, what do you suppose the license is worth? Do you know that the sheet of advertisements alone, at fivepence a line, brought in five hundred francs last month? You turn up the books, lad, and see what we make by placards and the registers at the Prefecture, and the work for the mayor's office, and the bishop too. You are a do-nothing that has no mind to get on. You are haggling over the horse that will carry you to some pretty bit of property like Marsac."

Attached to the valuation of plant there was a deed of partnership between Sechard senior and his son. The good father was to let his house and premises to the new firm for twelve hundred francs per annum, reserving one of the two rooms in the roof for himself. So long as David's purchase-money was not paid in full, the profits were to be divided equally; as soon as he paid off his father, he was to be made sole proprietor of the business.

David made a mental calculation of the value of the license, the goodwill, and the stock of paper, leaving the plant out of account. It was just possible, he thought, to clear off the debt. He accepted the conditions. Old Sechard, accustomed to peasants' haggling, knowing nothing of the wider business views of Paris, was amazed at such a prompt conclusion.

"Can he have been putting money by?" he asked himself. "Or is he scheming out, at this moment, some way of not paying me?"

With this notion in his head, he tried to find out whether David had any money with him; he wanted to be paid something on account. The old man's inquisitiveness roused his son's distrust; David remained close buttoned up to the chin.

Next day, old Sechard made the apprentice move all his own household stuff up into the attic until such time as an empty market cart could take it out on the return journey into the country; and David entered into possession of three bare, unfurnished rooms on the day that saw him installed in the printing-house, without one sou wherewith to pay his men's wages. When he asked his father, as a partner, to contribute his share towards the working expenses, the old man pretended not to understand. He had found the printing-house, he said, and he was not bound to find the money too. He had paid his share. Pressed close by his son's reasoning, he answered that when he himself had paid Rouzeau's widow he had not had a penny left. If he, a poor, ignorant working man, had made his way, Didot's apprentice should do still better. Besides, had not David been earning money, thanks to an education paid for by the sweat of his old father's brow? Now surely was the time when the education would come in useful.

"What have you done with your 'polls?'" he asked, returning to the charge. He meant to have light on a problem which his son left unresolved the day before.

"Why, had I not to live?" David asked indignantly, "and books to buy besides?"

"Oh! you bought books, did you? You will make a poor man of business. A man that buys books is hardly fit to print them," retorted the "bear."

Then David endured the most painful of humiliations – the sense of shame for a parent; there was nothing for it but to be passive while his father poured out a flood of reasons – sordid, whining, contemptible, money-getting reasons – in which the niggardly old man wrapped his refusal. David crushed down his pain into the depths of his soul; he saw that he was alone; saw that he had no one to look to but himself; saw, too, that his father was trying to make money out of him; and in a spirit of philosophical curiosity, he tried to find out how far the old man would go. He called old Sechard's attention to the fact that he had never as yet made any inquiry as to his mother's fortune; if that fortune would not buy the printing-house, it might go some ways towards paying the working expenses.

"Your mother's fortune?" echoed old Sechard; "why, it was her beauty and intelligence!"

David understood his father thoroughly after that answer; he understood that only after an interminable, expensive, and disgraceful lawsuit could he obtain any account of the money which by rights was his. The noble heart accepted the heavy burden laid upon it, seeing clearly beforehand how difficult it would be to free himself from the engagements into which he had entered with his father.

"I will work," he said to himself. "After all, if I have a rough time of it, so had the old man; besides, I shall be working for myself, shall I not?"

"I am leaving you a treasure," said Sechard, uneasy at his son's silence.

David asked what the treasure might be.

"Marion!" said his father.

Marion, a big country girl, was an indispensable part of the establishment. It was Marion who damped the paper and cut it to size; Marion did the cooking, washing, and marketing; Marion unloaded the paper carts, collected accounts, and cleaned the ink-balls; and if Marion had but known how to read, old Sechard would have put her to set up type into the bargain.

Old Sechard set out on foot for the country. Delighted as he was with his sale of the business, he was not quite easy in his mind as to the payment. To the throes of the vendor, the agony of uncertainty as to the completion of the purchase inevitably succeeds. Passion of every sort is essentially Jesuitical. Here was a man who thought that education was useless, forcing himself to believe in the influence of education. He was mortgaging thirty thousand francs upon the ideas of honor and conduct which education should have developed in his son; David had received a good training, so David would sweat blood and water to fulfil his engagements; David's knowledge would discover new resources; and David seemed to be full of fine feelings, so – David would pay! Many a parent does in this way, and thinks that he has acted a father's part; old Sechard was quite of that opinion by the time that he had reached his vineyard at Marsac, a hamlet some four leagues out of Angouleme. The previous owner had built a nice little house on the bit of property, and from year to year had added other bits of land to it, until in 1809 the old "bear" bought the whole, and went thither, exchanging the toil of the printing press for the labor of the winepress. As he put it himself, "he had been in that line so long that he ought to know something about it."

During the first twelvemonth of rural retirement, Sechard senior showed a careful countenance among his vine props; for he was always in his vineyard now, just as, in the old days, he had lived in his shop, day in, day out. The prospect of thirty thousand francs was even more intoxicating than sweet wine; already in imagination he fingered the coin. The less the claim to the money, the more eager he grew to pouch it. Not seldom his anxieties sent him hurrying from Marsac to Angouleme; he would climb up the rocky staircases into the old city and walk into his son's workshop to see how business went. There stood the presses in their places; the one apprentice, in a paper cap, was cleaning the ink-balls; there was a creaking of a press over the printing of some trade circular, the old type was still unchanged, and in the dens at the end of the room he saw his son and the foreman reading books, which the "bear" took for proof-sheets. Then he would join David at dinner and go back to Marsac, chewing the cud of uneasy reflection.

Avarice, like love, has the gift of second sight, instinctively guessing at future contingencies, and hugging its presentiments. Sechard senior living at a distance, far from the workshop and the machinery which possessed such a fascination for him, reminding him, as it did, of days when he was making his way, could *feel* that there were disquieting symptoms of inactivity in his son. The name of Cointet Brothers haunted him like a dread; he saw Sechard & Son dropping into the second place. In short, the old man scented misfortune in the wind.

His presentiments were too well founded; disaster was hovering over the house of Sechard. But there is a tutelary deity for misers, and by a chain of unforeseen circumstances that tutelary deity was so ordering matters that the purchase-money of his extortionate bargain was to be tumbled after all into the old toper's pouch.

Indifferent to the religious reaction brought about by the Restoration, indifferent no less to the Liberal movement, David preserved a most unlucky neutrality on the burning questions of the day. In those times provincial men of business were bound to profess political opinions of some sort if they meant to secure custom; they were forced to choose for themselves between the patronage of the Liberals on the one hand or the Royalists on the other. And Love, moreover, had come to David's heart, and with his scientific preoccupation and finer nature he had not room for the dogged greed of which our successful man of business is made; it choked the keen money-getting instinct which would have led him to study the differences between the Paris trade and the business of a provincial printing-house. The shades of opinion so sharply defined in the country are blurred and lost in the great currents of Parisian business life. Cointet Brothers set themselves deliberately to assimilate all shades of monarchical opinion. They let every one know that they fasted of a Friday and kept Lent; they haunted the cathedral; they cultivated the society of the clergy; and in consequence, when books of devotion were once more in demand, Cointet Brothers were the first in this lucrative field. They slandered David, accusing him of Liberalism, Atheism, and what not. How, asked they, could any one employ a man whose father had been a Septembrist, a Bonapartist, and a drunkard to boot? The old man was sure to leave plenty of gold pieces behind him. They themselves were poor men with families to support, while David was a bachelor and could do as he pleased; he would have plenty one of these days; he could afford to take things easily; whereas . . . and so forth and so forth.

Such tales against David, once put into circulation, produced their effect. The monopoly of the prefectorial and diocesan work passed gradually into the hands of Cointet Brothers; and before long David's keen competitors, emboldened by his inaction, started a second local sheet of advertisements and announcements. The older establishment was left at length with the job-printing orders from the town, and the circulation of the *Charente Chronicle* fell off by one-half. Meanwhile the Cointets grew richer; they had made handsome profits on their devotional books; and now they offered to buy Sechard's paper, to have all the trade and judicial announcements of the department in their own hands.

The news of this proposal sent by David to his father brought the old vinegrower from Marsac into the Place du Murier with the swiftness of the raven that scents the corpses on a battlefield.

"Leave me to manage the Cointets," said he to his son; "don't you meddle in this business."

The old man saw what the Cointets meant; and they took alarm at his clearsighted sagacity. His son was making a blunder, he said, and he, Sechard, had come to put a stop to it.

"What was to become of the connection if David gave up the paper? It all depended upon the paper. All the attorneys and solicitors and men of business in L'Houmeau were Liberals to a man. The Cointets had tried to ruin the Sechards by accusing them of Liberalism, and by so doing gave them a plank to cling to – the Sechards should keep the Liberal business. Sell the paper indeed! Why, you might as well sell the stock-in-trade and the license!"

Old Sechard asked the Cointets sixty thousand francs for the printing business, so as not to ruin his son; he was fond of his son; he was taking his son's part. The vinegrower brought his son to the front to gain his point, as a peasant brings in his wife.

His son was unwilling to do this, that, or the other; it varied according to the offers which he wrung one after another from the Cointets, until, not without an effort, he drew them on to give twenty-two thousand francs for the *Charente Chronicle*. But, at the same time, David must pledge himself thenceforward to print no newspaper whatsoever, under a penalty of thirty thousand francs for damages.

That transaction dealt the deathblow to the Sechard establishment; but the old vinegrower did not trouble himself much on that head. Murder usually follows robbery. Our worthy friend intended to pay himself with the ready money. To have the cash in his own hands he would have given in David himself over and above the bargain, and so much the more willingly since that this nuisance of a son could claim one-half of the unexpected windfall. Taking this fact into consideration, therefore, the generous parent consented to abandon his share of the business but not the business premises; and the rental was still maintained at the famous sum of twelve hundred francs per annum.

The old man came into town very seldom after the paper was sold to the Cointets. He pleaded his advanced age, but the truth was that he took little interest in the establishment now that it was his no longer. Still, he could not quite shake off his old kindness for his stock-in-trade; and when business brought him into Angouleme, it would have been hard to say which was the stronger attraction to the old house – his wooden presses or the son whom (as a matter of form) he asked for rent. The old foreman, who had gone over to the rival establishment, knew exactly how much this fatherly generosity was worth; the old fox meant to reserve a right to interfere in his son's affairs, and had taken care to appear in the bankruptcy as a privileged creditor for arrears of rent.

The causes of David's heedlessness throw a light on the character of that young man. Only a few days after his establishment in the paternal printing office, he came across an old school friend in the direst poverty. Lucien Chardon, a young fellow of one-and-twenty or thereabouts, was the son of a surgeon-major who had retired with a wound from the republican army. Nature had meant M. Chardon senior for a chemist; chance opened the way for a retail druggist's business in Angouleme. After many years of scientific research, death cut him off in the midst of his incompleted experiments, and the great discovery that should have brought wealth to the family was never made. Chardon had tried to find a specific for the gout. Gout is a rich man's malady; the rich will pay large sums to recover health when they have lost it, and for this reason the druggist deliberately selected gout as his problem. Halfway between the man of science on the one side and the charlatan on the other, he saw that the scientific method was the one road to assured success, and had studied the causes of the complaint, and based his remedy on a certain general theory of treatment, with modifications in practice for varying temperaments. Then, on a visit to Paris undertaken to solicit the approval of the *Academie des Sciences*, he died, and lost all the fruits of his labors.

It may have been that some presentiment of the end had led the country druggist to do all that in him lay to give his boy and girl a good education; the family had been living up to the income brought in by the business; and now when they were left almost destitute, it was an aggravation of their misfortune that they had been brought up in the expectations of a brilliant future; for these hopes were extinguished by their father's death. The great Desplein, who attended Chardon in his last illness, saw him die in convulsions of rage.

The secret of the army surgeon's ambition lay in his passionate love for his wife, the last survivor of the family of Rubempre, saved as by a miracle from the guillotine in 1793. He had gained time by declaring that she was pregnant, a lie told without the girl's knowledge or consent. Then, when in a manner he had created a claim to call her his wife, he had married her in spite of their common poverty. The children of this marriage, like all children of love, inherited the mother's wonderful beauty, that gift so often fatal when accompanied by poverty. The life of hope and hard work and despair, in all of which Mme. Chardon had shared with such keen sympathy, had left deep traces in her beautiful face, just as the slow decline of a scanty income had changed her ways and habits; but both she and her children confronted evil days bravely enough. She sold the druggist's shop in the Grand' Rue de L'Houmeau, the principal suburb of Angouleme; but it was impossible for even one woman to exist on the three hundred francs of income brought in by the investment of the purchase-money, so the mother and daughter accepted the position, and worked to earn a living. The mother went out as a monthly nurse, and for her gentle manners was preferred to any other among the wealthy houses, where she lived without expense to her children, and earned some seven francs a week. To save her son the embarrassment of seeing his mother reduced to this humble position, she assumed the name of Madame Charlotte; and persons requiring her services were requested to apply to M. Postel, M. Chardon's successor in the business. Lucien's sister worked for a laundress, a decent woman much respected in L'Houmeau, and earned fifteen daily sous. As Mme. Prieur's forewoman she had a certain position in the workroom, which raised her slightly above the class of working-girls.

The two women's slender earnings, together with Mme. Chardon's three hundred francs of *rentes*, amounted to about eight hundred francs a year, and on this sum three persons must be fed, clothed, and lodged. Yet, with all their frugal thrift, the pittance was scarcely sufficient; nearly the whole of it was needed for Lucien. Mme. Chardon and her daughter Eve believed in Lucien as Mahomet's wife believed in her husband; their devotion for his future knew no bounds. Their present landlord was the successor to the business, for M. Postel let them have rooms at the further end of a yard at the back of the laboratory for a very low rent, and Lucien slept in the poor garret above. A father's passion for natural science had stimulated the boy, and at first induced him to follow in the same path. Lucien was one of the most brilliant pupils at the grammar school of Angouleme, and when David Sechard left, his future friend was in the third form.

When chance brought the school-fellows together again, Lucien was weary of drinking from the rude cup of penury, and ready for any of the rash, decisive steps that youth takes at the age of twenty. David's generous offer of forty francs a month if Lucien would come to him and learn the work of a printer's reader came in time; David had no need whatever of a printer's reader, but he saved Lucien from despair. The ties of a school friendship thus renewed were soon drawn closer than ever by the similarity of their lot in life and the dissimilarity of their characters. Both felt high swelling hopes of manifold success; both consciously possessed the high order of intelligence which sets a man on a level with lofty heights, consigned though they were socially to the lowest level. Fate's injustice was a strong bond between them. And then, by different ways, following each his own bent of mind, they had attained to poesy. Lucien, destined for the highest speculative fields of natural science, was aiming with hot enthusiasm at fame through literature; while David, with that meditative temperament which inclines to poetry, was drawn by his tastes towards natural science.

The exchange of roles was the beginning of an intellectual comradeship. Before long, Lucien told David of his own father's farsighted views of the application of science to manufacture, while David pointed out the new ways in literature that Lucien must follow if he meant to succeed. Not many days had passed before the young men's friendship became a passion such as is only known in early manhood. Then it was that David caught a glimpse of Eve's fair face, and loved, as grave and meditative natures can love. The *et nunc et semper et in secula seculorum* of the Liturgy is the device taken by many a sublime unknown poet, whose works consist in magnificent epics conceived and lost between heart and heart. With a lover's insight, David read the secret hopes set by the mother and sister on Lucien's poet's brow; and knowing their blind devotion, it was very sweet to him to draw nearer to his love by sharing her hopes and her self-sacrifice. And in this way Lucien came to be David's chosen brother. As there are ultras who would fain be more Royalist than the King, so David outdid the mother and sister in his belief in Lucien's genius; he spoiled Lucien as a mother spoils her child.

Once, under pressure of the lack of money which tied their hands, the two were ruminating after the manner of young men over ways of promptly realizing a large fortune; and, after fruitless shakings of all the trees already stripped by previous comers, Lucien bethought himself of two of his father's ideas. M. Chardon had talked of a method of refining sugar by a chemical process, which would reduce the cost of production by one-half; and he had another plan for employing an American vegetable fibre for making paper, something after the Chinese fashion, and effecting an enormous saving in the cost of raw material. David, knowing the importance of a question raised already by the Didots, caught at this latter notion, saw a fortune in it, and looked upon Lucien as the benefactor whom he could never repay.

Any one may guess how the ruling thoughts and inner life of this pair of friends unfitted them for carrying on the business of a printing house. So far from making fifteen to twenty thousand francs, like Cointet Brothers, printers and publishers to the diocese, and proprietors of the *Charente Chronicle1* – Sechard & Son made a bare three hundred francs per month, out of which the foreman's salary must be paid, as well as Marion's wages and the rent and taxes; so that David himself was scarcely making twelve hundred francs per annum. Active and industrious men of business would have bought new type and new machinery, and made an effort to secure orders for cheap printing from the Paris book trade; but master and foreman, deep in absorbing intellectual interests, were quite content with such orders as came to them from their remaining customers.

In the long length the Cointets had come to understand David's character and habits. They did not slander him now; on the contrary, wise policy required that they should allow the business to flicker on; it was to their interest indeed to maintain it in a small way, lest it should fall into the hands of some more formidable competitor; they made a practice of sending prospectuses and circulars – job-printing, as it is called – to the Sechard's establishment. So it came about that, all unwittingly, David owed his existence, commercially speaking, to the cunning schemes of his competitors. The Cointets, well pleased with his "craze," as they called it, behaved to all appearance both fairly and handsomely; but, as a matter of fact, they were adopting the tactics of the mail-coach owners who set up a sham opposition coach to keep *bona fide* rivals out of the field.

Inside and outside, the condition of the Sechard printing establishment bore testimony to the sordid avarice of the old "bear," who never spent a penny on repairs. The old house had stood in sun and rain, and borne the brunt of the weather, till it looked like some venerable tree trunk set down at the entrance of the alley, so riven it was with seams and cracks of all sorts and sizes. The house front, built of brick and stone, with no pretensions to symmetry, seemed to be bending beneath the weight of a worm-eaten roof covered with the curved pantiles in common use in the South of France. The decrepit casements were fitted with the heavy, unwieldy shutters necessary in that climate, and held in place by massive iron cross bars. It would have puzzled you to find a more dilapidated house in Angouleme; nothing but sheer tenacity of mortar kept it together. Try to picture the workshop, lighted at either end, and dark in the middle; the walls covered with handbills and begrimed by friction of all the workmen who had rubbed past them for thirty years; the cobweb of cordage across the ceiling, the stacks of paper, the old-fashioned presses, the pile of slabs for weighting the damp sheets, the rows of cases, and the two dens in the far corners where the master printer and foreman sat – and you will have some idea of the life led by the two friends.

One day early in May, 1821, David and Lucien were standing together by the window that looked into the yard. It was nearly two o'clock, and the four or five men were going out to dinner. David waited until the apprentice had shut the street door with the bell fastened to it; then he drew Lucien out into the yard as if the smell of paper, ink, and presses and old woodwork had grown intolerable to him, and together they sat down under the vines, keeping the office and the door in view. The sunbeams, playing among the trellised vine-shoots, hovered over the two poets, making, as it were, an aureole about their heads, bringing the contrast between their faces and their characters into a vigorous relief that would have tempted the brush of some great painter.

David's physique was of the kind that Nature gives to the fighter, the man born to struggle in obscurity, or with the eyes of all men turned upon him. The strong shoulders, rising above the broad chest, were in keeping with the full development of his whole frame. With his thick crop of black hair, his fleshy, high-colored, swarthy face, supported by a thick neck, he looked at first sight like one of Boileau's canons: but on a second glance there was that in the lines about the thick lips, in the dimple of the chin, in the turn of the square nostrils, with the broad irregular line of central cleavage, and, above all, in the eyes, with the steady light of an all-absorbing love that burned in them, which revealed the real character of the man – the wisdom of the thinker, the strenuous melancholy of a spirit that discerns the horizon on either side, and sees clearly to the end of winding ways, turning the clear light of analysis upon the joys of fruition, known as yet in idea alone, and quick to turn from them in disgust. You might look for the flash of genius from such a face; you could not miss the ashes of the volcano; hopes extinguished beneath a profound sense of the social annihilation to which lowly birth and lack of fortune condemns so many a loftier mind. And by the side of the poor printer, who loathed a handicraft so closely allied to intellectual work, close to this Silenus, joyless, self-sustained, drinking deep draughts from the cup of knowledge and of poetry that he might forget the cares of his narrow lot in the intoxication of soul and brain, stood Lucien, graceful as some sculptured Indian Bacchus.

For in Lucien's face there was the distinction of line which stamps the beauty of the antique; the Greek profile, with the velvet whiteness of women's faces, and eyes full of love, eyes so blue that they looked dark against a pearly setting, and dewy and fresh as those of a child. Those beautiful eyes looked out from under their long chestnut lashes, beneath eyebrows that might have been traced by a Chinese pencil. The silken down on his cheeks, like his bright curling hair, shone golden in the sunlight. A divine graciousness transfused the white temples that caught that golden gleam; a matchless nobleness had set its seal in the short chin raised, but not abruptly. The smile that hovered about the coral lips, yet redder as they seemed by force of contrast with the even teeth, was the smile of some sorrowing angel. Lucien's hands denoted race; they were shapely hands; hands that men obey at a sign, and women love to kiss. Lucien was slender and of middle height. From a glance at his feet, he might have been taken for a girl in disguise, and this so much the more easily from the feminine contour of the hips, a characteristic of keen-witted, not to say, astute, men. This is a trait which seldom misleads, and in Lucien it was a true indication of character; for when he analyzed the society of to-day, his restless mind was apt to take its stand on the lower ground of those diplomatists who hold that success justifies the use of any means however base. It is one of the misfortunes attendant upon great intellects that perforce they comprehend all things, both good and evil.

The two young men judged society by the more lofty standard because their social position was at the lowest end of the scale, for unrecognized power is apt to avenge itself for lowly station by viewing the world from a lofty standpoint. Yet it is, nevertheless, true that they grew but the more bitter and hopeless after these swift soaring flights to the upper regions of thought, their world by right. Lucien had read much and compared; David had thought much and deeply. In spite of the young printer's look of robust, country-bred health, his turn of mind was melancholy and somewhat morbid – he lacked confidence in himself; but Lucien, on the other hand, with a boldness little to be expected from his feminine, almost effeminate, figure, graceful though it was, Lucien possessed the Gascon temperament to the highest degree – rash, brave, and adventurous, prone to make the most of the bright side, and as little as possible of the dark; his was the nature that sticks at no crime if there is anything to be gained by it, and laughs at the vice which serves as a stepping-stone. Just now these tendencies of ambition were held in check, partly by the fair illusions of youth, partly by the enthusiasm which led him to prefer the nobler methods, which every man in love with glory tries first of all. Lucien was struggling as yet with himself and his own desires, and not with the difficulties of life; at strife with his own power, and not with the baseness of other men, that fatal exemplar for impressionable minds. The brilliancy of his intellect had a keen attraction for David. David admired his friend, while he kept him out of the scrapes into which he was led by the *furie francaise*.

David, with his well-balanced mind and timid nature at variance with a strong constitution, was by no means wanting in the persistence of the Northern temper; and if he saw all the difficulties before him, none the less he vowed to himself to conquer, never to give way. In him the unswerving virtue of an apostle was softened by pity that sprang from inexhaustible indulgence. In the friendship grown old already, one was the worshiper, and that one was David; Lucien ruled him like a woman sure of love, and David loved to give way. He felt that his friend's physical beauty implied a real superiority, which he accepted, looking upon himself as one made of coarser and commoner human clay.

"The ox for patient labor in the fields, the free life for the bird," he thought to himself. "I will be the ox, and Lucien shall be the eagle."

So for three years these friends had mingled the destinies bright with such glorious promise. Together they read the great works that appeared above the horizon of literature and science since the Peace – the poems of Schiller, Goethe, and Byron, the prose writings of Scott, Jean-Paul, Berzelius, Davy, Cuvier, Lamartine, and many more. They warmed themselves beside these great hearthfires; they tried their powers in abortive creations, in work laid aside and taken up again with new glow of enthusiasm. Incessantly they worked with the unwearied vitality of youth; comrades in poverty, comrades in the consuming love of art and science, till they forgot the hard life of the present, for their minds were wholly bent on laying the foundations of future fame.

"Lucien," said David, "do you know what I have just received from Paris?" He drew a tiny volume from his pocket. "Listen!"

And David read, as a poet can read, first Andre de Chenier's Idyll *Neere*, then *Le Malade*, following on with the Elegy on a Suicide, another elegy in the classic taste, and the last two *Iambes*.

"So that is Andre de Chenier!" Lucien ex-claimed again and again. "It fills one with despair!" he cried for the third time, when David surrendered the book to him, unable to read further for emotion. – "A poet redis-covered by a poet!" said Lucien, reading the signature of the preface.

"After Chenier had written those poems, he thought that he had written nothing worth publishing," added David.

Then Lucien in his turn read aloud the frag-ment of an epic called *L'Aveugle* and two or three of the Elegies, till, when he came upon the line–

If they know not bliss, is there happiness on earth?

He pressed the book to his lips, and tears came to the eyes of either, for the two friends were lovers and fellow-worshipers.

The vine-stems were changing color with the spring; covering the rifted, battered walls of the old house where squalid cracks were spreading in every direction, with fluted columns and knots and bas-reliefs and un-counted masterpieces of I know not what or-der of architecture, erected by fairy hands. Fancy had scattered flowers and crimson gems over the gloomy little yard, and Chenier's

Camille became for David the Eve whom he worshiped, for Lucien a great lady to whom he paid his homage. Poetry had shaken out her starry robe above the workshop where the "monkeys" and "bears" were grotesquely busy among types and presses. Five o'clock struck, but the friends felt neither hunger nor thirst; life had turned to a golden dream, and all the treasures of the world lay at their feet. Far away on the horizon lay the blue streak to which Hope points a finger in storm and stress; and a siren voice sounded in their ears, calling, "Come, spread your wings; through that streak of gold or silver or azure lies the sure way of escape from evil fortune!"

Just at that moment the low glass door of the workshop was opened, and out came Cerizet, an apprentice (David had brought the urchin from Paris). This youth introduced a stranger, who saluted the friends politely, and spoke to David

"This, sir, is a monograph which I am desirous of printing," said he, drawing a huge package of manuscript from his pocket. "Will you oblige me with an estimate?"

"We do not undertake work on such a scale, sir," David answered, without looking at the manuscript. "You had better see the Messieurs Cointet about it."

"Still we have a very pretty type which might suit it," put in Lucien, taking up the roll. "We must ask you to be kind enough, sir, to leave your commission with us and call again to-morrow, and we will give you an estimate."

"Have I the pleasure of addressing M. Lucien Chardon?"

"Yes, sir," said the foreman.

"I am fortunate in this opportunity of meeting with a young poet destined to such greatness," returned the author. "Mme. de Bargeton sent me here."

Lucien flushed red at the name, and stammered out something about gratitude for the interest which Mme. de Bargeton took in him. David noticed his friend's embarrassed flush, and left him in conversation with the country gentleman, the author of a monograph on silkwork cultivation, prompted by vanity to print the effort for the benefit of fellow-members of the local agricultural society.

When the author had gone, David spoke.

"Lucien, are you in love with Mme. de Bargeton?"

"Passionately."

"But social prejudices set you as far apart as if she were living at Pekin and you in Greenland."

"The will of two lovers can rise victorious over all things," said Lucien, lowering his eyes.

"You will forget us," returned the alarmed lover, as Eve's fair face rose before his mind.

"On the contrary, I have perhaps sacrificed my love to you," cried Lucien.

"What do you mean?"

"In spite of my love, in spite of the different motives which bid me obtain a secure footing in her house, I have told her that I will never go thither again unless another is made welcome too, a man whose gifts are greater than mine, a man destined for a brilliant future – David Sechard, my brother, my friend. I shall find an answer waiting when I go home. All the aristocrats may have been asked to hear me read my verses this evening, but I shall not go if the answer is negative, and I will never set foot in Mme. de Bargeton's house again."

David brushed the tears from his eyes, and wrung Lucien's hand. The clock struck six.

"Eve must be anxious; good-bye," Lucien added abruptly.

He hurried away. David stood overcome by the emotion that is only felt to the full at his age, and more especially in such a position as his – the friends were like two young swans with wings unclipped as yet by the experiences of provincial life.

"Heart of gold!" David exclaimed to himself, as his eyes followed Lucien across the workshop.

Lucien went down to L'Houmeau along the broad Promenade de Beaulieu, the Rue du Minage, and Saint-Peter's Gate. It was the longest way round, so you may be sure that Mme. de Bargeton's house lay on the way. So delicious it was to pass under her windows, though she knew nothing of his presence, that for the past two months he had gone round daily by the Palet Gate into L'Houmeau.

Under the trees of Beaulieu he saw how far the suburb lay from the city. The custom of the country, moreover, had raised other barriers harder to surmount than the mere physical difficulty of the steep flights of steps which Lucien was descending. Youth and ambition had thrown the flying-bridge of glory across the gulf between the city and the suburb, yet Lucien was as uneasy in his mind over his lady's answer as any king's favorite who has tried to climb yet higher, and fears that being over-bold he is like to fall. This must seem a dark saying to those who have never studied the manners and customs of cities divided into the upper and lower town; wherefore it is necessary to enter here upon some topographical details, and this so much the more if the reader is to comprehend the position of one of the principal characters in the story – Mme. de Bargeton.

The old city of Angouleme is perched aloft on a crag like a sugar-loaf, overlooking the plain where the Charente winds away through the meadows. The crag is an outlying spur on the Perigord side of a long, low ridge of hill, which terminates abruptly just above the road from Paris to Bordeaux, so that the Rock of Angouleme is a sort of promontory marking out the line of three picturesque valleys. The ramparts and great gateways and ruined fortress on the summit of the crag still remain to bear witness to the importance of this stronghold during the Religious Wars, when Angouleme was a military position coveted alike of Catholics and Calvinists, but its old-world strength is a source of weakness in modern days; Angouleme could not spread down to the Charente, and shut in between its ramparts and the steep sides of the crag, the old town is condemned to stagnation of the most fatal kind.

The Government made an attempt about this very time to extend the town towards Perigord, building a Prefecture, a Naval School, and barracks along the hillside, and opening up roads. But private enterprise had been beforehand elsewhere. For some time past the suburb of L'Houmeau had sprung up, a mushroom growth at the foot of the crag and along the river-side, where the direct road runs from Paris to Bordeaux. Everybody has heard of the great paper-mills of Angouleme, established perforce three hundred years ago on the Charente and its branch streams, where there was a sufficient fall of water. The largest State factory of marine ordnance in France was established at Ruelle, some six miles away. Carriers, wheelwrights, posthouses, and inns, every agency for public conveyance, every industry that lives by road or river, was crowded together in Lower Angouleme, to avoid the difficulty of the ascent of the hill. Naturally, too, tanneries, laundries, and all such waterside trades stood within reach of the Charente; and along the banks of the river lay the stores of brandy and great warehouses full of the water-borne raw material; all the carrying trade of the Charente, in short, had lined the quays with buildings.

So the Faubourg of L'Houmeau grew into a busy and prosperous city, a second Angouleme rivaling the upper town, the residence of the powers that be, the lords spiritual and temporal of Angouleme; though L'Houmeau, with all its business and increasing greatness, was still a mere appendage of the city above. The *noblesse* and officialdom dwelt on the crag, trade and wealth remained below. No love was lost between these two sections of the community all the world over, and in Angouleme it would have been hard to say which of the two camps detested the other the more cordially. Under the Empire the machinery worked fairly smoothly, but the Restoration wrought both sides to the highest pitch of exasperation.

Nearly every house in the upper town of Angouleme is inhabited by noble, or at any rate by old burgher, families, who live independently on their incomes – a sort of autochthonous nation who suffer no aliens to come among them. Possibly, after two hundred years of unbroken residence, and it may be an intermarriage or two with one of the primordial houses, a family from some neighboring district may be adopted, but in the eyes of the aboriginal race they are still newcomers of yesterday.

Prefects, receivers-general, and various administrations that have come and gone during the last forty years, have tried to tame the ancient families perched aloft like wary ravens on their crag; the said families were always willing to accept invitations to dinners and dances; but as to admitting the strangers to their own houses, they were inexorable. Ready to scoff and disparage, jealous and niggardly, marrying only among themselves, the families formed a serried phalanx to keep out intruders. Of modern luxury they had no notion; and as for sending a boy to Paris, it was sending him, they thought to certain ruin. Such sagacity will give a sufficient idea of the old-world manners and customs of this society, suffering from thick-headed Royalism, infected with bigotry rather than zeal, all stagnating together, motionless as their town founded upon a rock. Yet Angouleme enjoyed a great reputation in the provinces round about for its educational advantages, and neighboring towns sent their daughters to its boarding schools and convents.

It is easy to imagine the influence of the class sentiment which held Angouleme aloof from L'Houmeau. The merchant classes are rich, the *noblesse* are usually poor. Each side takes its revenge in scorn of the other. The tradespeople in Angouleme espouse the quarrel. "He is a man of L'Houmeau!" a shopkeeper of the upper town will tell you, speaking of a merchant in the lower suburb, throwing an accent into the speech which no words can describe. When the Restoration defined the position of the French *noblesse*, holding out hopes to them which could only be realized by a complete and general topsy-turvy-dom, the distance between Angouleme and L'Houmeau, already more strongly marked than the distance between the hill and plain, was widened yet further. The better families, all devoted as one man to the Government, grew more exclusive here than in any other part of France. "The man of L'Houmeau" became little better than a pariah. Hence the deep, smothered hatred which broke out everywhere with such ugly unanimity in the insurrection of 1830 and destroyed the elements of a durable social system in France. As the overweening haughtiness of the Court nobles detached the provincial *noblesse* from the throne, so did these last alienate the *bourgeoisie* from the royal cause by behavior that galled their vanity in every possible way.

So "a man of L'Houmeau," a druggist's son, in Mme. de Bargeton's house was nothing less than a little revolution. Who was responsible for it? Lamartine and Victor Hugo, Casimir Delavigne and Canalis, Beranger and Chateaubriand. Davrigny, Benjamin Constant and Lamennais, Cousin and Michaud, – all the old and young illustrious names in literature in short, Liberals and Royalists, alike must divide the blame among them. Mme. de Bargeton loved art and letters, eccentric taste on her part, a craze deeply deplored in Angouleme. In justice to the lady, it is necessary to give a sketch of the previous history of a woman born to shine, and left by unlucky circumstances in the shade, a woman whose influence decided Lucien's career.

M. de Bargeton was the great-grandson of an alderman of Bordeaux named Mirault, ennobled under Louis XIII. for long tenure of office. His son, bearing the name of Mirault de Bargeton, became an officer in the household troops of Louis XIV., and married so great a fortune that in the reign of Louis XV. his son dropped the

Mirault and was called simply M. de Bargeton. This M. de Bargeton, the alderman's grandson, lived up to his quality so strenuously that he ran through the family property and checked the course of its fortunes. Two of his brothers indeed, great-uncles of the present Bargeton, went into business again, for which reason you will find the name of Mirault among Bordeaux merchants at this day. The lands of Bargeton, in Angoumois in the barony of Rochefoucauld, being entailed, and the house in Angouleme, called the Hotel Bargeton, likewise, the grandson of M. de Bargeton the Waster came in for these hereditaments; though the year 1789 deprived him of all seignorial rights save to the rents paid by his tenants, which amounted to some ten thousand francs per annum. If his grandsire had but walked in the ways of his illustrious progenitors, Bargeton I. and Bargeton II., Bargeton V. (who may be dubbed Bargeton the Mute by way of distinction) should by rights have been born to the title of Marquis of Bargeton; he would have been connected with some great family or other, and in due time he would have been a duke and a peer of France, like many another; whereas, in 1805, he thought himself uncommonly lucky when he married Mlle. Marie-Louise-Anais de Negrepelisse, the daughter of a noble long relegated to the obscurity of his manor-house, scion though he was of the younger branch of one of the oldest families in the south of France. There had been a Negrepelisse among the hostages of St. Louis.

The head of the elder branch, however, had borne the illustrious name of d'Espard since the reign of Henri Quatre, when the Negrepelisse of that day married an heiress of the d'Espard family. As for M. de Negrepelisse, the younger son of a younger son, he lived upon his wife's property, a small estate in the neighborhood of Barbezieux, farming the land to admiration, selling his corn in the market himself, and distilling his own brandy, laughing at those who ridiculed him, so long as he could pile up silver crowns, and now and again round out his estate with another bit of land.

Circumstances unusual enough in out-of-the-way places in the country had inspired Mme. de Bargeton with a taste for music and reading. During the Revolution one Abbe Niollant, the Abbe Roze's best pupil, found a hiding-place in the old manor-house of Escarbas, and brought with him his baggage of musical compositions. The old country gentleman's hospitality was handsomely repaid, for the Abbe undertook his daughter's education. Anais, or Nais, as she was called must otherwise have been left to herself, or, worse still, to some coarse-minded servant-maid. The Abbe was not only a musician, he was well and widely read, and knew both Italian and German; so Mlle. de Negrepelise received instruction in those tongues, as well as in counterpoint. He explained the great masterpieces of the French, German, and Italian literatures, and deciphered with her the music of the great composers. Finally, as time hung heavy on his hands in the seclusion enforced by political storms, he taught his pupil Latin and Greek and some smatterings of natural science. A mother might have modified the effects of a man's education upon a young girl, whose independent spirit had been fostered in the first place by a country life. The Abbe Niollant, an enthusiast and a poet, possessed the artistic temperament in a peculiarly high degree, a temperament compatible with many estimable qualities, but prone to raise itself above *bourgeois* prejudices by the liberty of its judgments and breadth of view. In society an intellect of this order wins pardon for its boldness by its depth and originality; but in private life it would seem to do positive mischief, by suggesting wanderings from the beaten track. The Abbe was by no means wanting in goodness of heart, and his ideas were therefore the more contagious for this high-spirited girl, in whom they were confirmed by a lonely life. The Abbe Niollant's pupil learned to be fearless in criticism and ready in judgement; it never occurred to her tutor that qualities so necessary in a man are disadvantages in a woman destined for the homely life of a house-mother. And though the Abbe constantly impressed it upon his pupil that it behoved her to be the more modest and gracious with the extent of her attainments, Mlle. de Negrepelisse conceived an excellent opinion of herself and a robust contempt for ordinary humanity. All those about her were her inferiors, or persons who hastened to do her bidding, till she grew to be as haughty as a great lady, with none of the charming blandness and urbanity of a great lady. The instincts of vanity were flattered by the pride that the poor Abbe took in his pupil, the pride of an author who sees himself in his work, and for her misfortune she met no one with whom she could measure herself. Isolation is one of the greatest drawbacks of a country life. We lose the habit of putting ourselves to any inconvenience for the sake of others when there is no one for whom to make the trifling sacrifices of personal effort required by dress and manner. And everything in us shares in the change for the worse; the form and the spirit deteriorate together.

With no social intercourse to compel self-repression, Mlle. de Negrepelisse's bold ideas passed into her manner and the expression of her face. There was a cavalier air about her, a something that seems at first original, but only suited to women of adventurous life. So this education, and the consequent asperities of character, which would have been softened down in a higher social sphere, could only serve to make her ridiculous at Angouleme so soon as her adorers should cease to worship eccentricities that charm only in youth.

As for M. de Negrepelisse, he would have given all his daughter's books to save the life of a sick bullock; and so miserly was he, that he would not have given her two farthings over and above the allowance to which she had a right, even if it had been a question of some indispensable trifle for her education.

In 1802 the Abbe died, before the marriage of his dear child, a marriage which he, doubtless, would never have advised. The old father found his daughter a great care now that the Abbe was gone. The high-spirited girl, with nothing else to do, was sure to break into rebellion against his niggardliness, and he felt quite unequal to the struggle. Like all young women who leave the appointed track of woman's life, Nais had her own opinions about marriage, and had no great inclination thereto. She shrank from submitting herself, body and soul, to the feeble, undignified specimens of mankind whom she had chanced to meet. She wished to rule, marriage meant obedience; and between obedience to coarse caprices and a mind without indulgence for her tastes, and flight with a lover who should please her, she would not have hesitated for a moment.

M. de Negrepelisse maintained sufficient of the tradition of birth to dread a *mesalliance*. Like many another parent, he resolved to marry his daughter, not so much on her account as for his own peace of mind. A noble or a country gentleman was the man for him, somebody not too clever, incapable of haggling over the account of the trust; stupid enough and easy enough to allow Nais to have her own way, and disinterested enough to take her without a dowry. But where to look for a son-in-law to suit father and daughter equally well, was the problem. Such a man would be the phoenix of sons-in-law.

To M. de Negrepelisse pondering over the eligible bachelors of the province with these double requirements in his mind. M. de Bargeton seemed to be the only one who answered to this description. M. de Bargeton, aged forty, considerably shattered by the amorous dissipations of his youth, was generally held to be a man of remarkably feeble intellect; but he had just the exact amount of commonsense required for the management of his fortune, and breeding sufficient to enable him to avoid blunders or blatant follies in society in Angouleme. In the bluntest manner M. de Negrepelisse pointed out the negative virtues of the model husband designed for his daughter, and made her see the way to manage him so as to secure her own happiness. So Nais married the bearer of arms, two hundred years old already, for the Bargeton arms are blazoned thus: *the first or, three attires gules; the second, three ox's heads cabossed, two and one, sable; the third, barry of six, azure and argent, in the first, six shells or, three, two, and one.* Provided with a chaperon, Nais could steer her fortunes as she chose under the style of the firm, and with the help of such connections as her wit and beauty would obtain for her in Paris. Nais was enchanted by the prospect of such liberty. M. de

Bargeton was of the opinion that he was making a brilliant marriage, for he expected that in no long while M. de Negrepelisse would leave him the estates which he was rounding out so lovingly; but to an unprejudiced spectator it certainly seemed as though the duty of writing the bridegroom's epitaph might devolve upon his father-in-law.

By this time Mme. de Bargeton was thirty-six years old and her husband fifty-eight. The disparity in age was the more startling since M. de Bargeton looked like a man of seventy, whereas his wife looked scarcely half her age. She could still wear rose-color, and her hair hanging loose upon her shoulders. Although their income did not exceed twelve thousand francs, they ranked among the half-dozen largest fortunes in the old city, merchants and officials excepted; for M. and Mme. de Bargeton were obliged to live in Angouleme until such time as Mme. de Bargeton's inheritance should fall in and they could go to Paris. Meanwhile they were bound to be attentive to old M. de Negrepelisse (who kept them waiting so long that his son-in-law in fact predeceased him), and Nais' brilliant intellectual gifts, and the wealth that lay like undiscovered ore in her nature, profited her nothing, underwent the transforming operation of Time and changed to absurdities. For our absurdities spring, in fact, for the most part, from the good in us, from some faculty or quality abnormally developed. Pride, untempered by intercourse with the great world becomes stiff and starched by contact with petty things; in a loftier moral atmosphere it would have grown to noble magnanimity. Enthusiasm, that virtue within a virtue, forming the saint, inspiring the devotion hidden from all eyes and glowing out upon the world in verse, turns to exaggeration, with the trifles of a narrow existence for its object. Far away from the centres of light shed by great minds, where the air is quick with thought, knowledge stands still, taste is corrupted like stagnant water, and passion dwindles, frittered away upon the infinitely small objects which it strives to exalt. Herein lies the secret of the avarice and tittle-tattle that poison provincial life. The contagion of narrow-mindedness and meanness affects the noblest natures; and in such ways as these, men born to be great, and women who would have been charming if they had fallen under the forming influence of greater minds, are balked of their lives.

Here was Mme. de Bargeton, for instance, smiting the lyre for every trifle, and publishing her emotions indiscriminately to her circle. As a matter of fact, when sensations appeal to an audience of one, it is better to keep them to ourselves. A sunset certainly is a glorious poem; but if a woman describes it, in high-sounding words, for the benefit of matter-of-fact people, is she not ridiculous? There are pleasures which can only be felt to the full when two souls meet, poet and poet, heart and heart. She had a trick of using high-sounding phrases, interlarded with exaggerated expressions, the kind of stuff ingeniously nicknamed *tartines* by the French journalist, who furnishes a daily supply of the commodity for a public that daily performs the difficult feat of swallowing it. She squandered superlatives recklessly in her talk, and the smallest things took giant proportions. It was at this period of her career that she began to type-ize, individualize, synthesize, dramatize, superiorize, analyze, poetize, angelize, neologize, tragedify, prosify, and colossify – you must violate the laws of language to find words to express the new-fangled whimsies in which even women here and there indulge. The heat of her language communicated itself to the brain, and the dithyrambs on her lips were spoken out of the abundance of her heart. She palpitated, swooned, and went into ecstasies over anything and everything, over the devotion of a sister of Charity, and the execution of the brothers Fauchet, over M. d'Arlincourt's *Ipsiboe*, Lewis' *Anaconda*, or the escape of La Valette, or the presence of mind of a lady friend who put burglars to flight by imitating a man's voice. Everything was heroic, extraordinary, strange, wonderful, and divine. She would work herself into a state of excitement, indignation, or depression; she soared to heaven, and sank again, gazed at the sky, or looked to earth; her eyes were always filled with tears. She wore herself out with chronic admiration, and wasted her strength on curious dislikes. Her mind ran on the Pasha of Janina; she would have liked to try conclusions with him in his seraglio, and had a great notion of being sewn in a sack and thrown into the water. She envied that blue-stocking of the desert, Lady Hester Stanhope; she longed to be a sister of Saint Camilla and tend the sick and die of yellow fever in a hospital at Barcelona; 'twas a high, a noble destiny! In short, she thirsted for any draught but the clear spring water of her own life, flowing hidden among green pastures. She adored Byron and Jean-Jacques Rousseau, or anybody else with a picturesque or dramatic career. Her tears were ready to flow for every misfortune; she sang paeans for every victory. She sympathized with the fallen Napoleon, and with Mehemet Ali, massacring the foreign usurpers of Egypt. In short, any kind of genius was accommodated with an aureole, and she was fully persuaded that gifted immortals lived on incense and light

A good many people looked upon her as a harmless lunatic, but in these extravagances of hers a keener observer surely would have seen the broken fragments of a magnificent edifice that had crumbled into ruin before it was completed, the stones of a heavenly Jerusalem – love, in short, without a lover. And this was indeed the fact.

The story of the first eighteen years of Mme. de Bargeton's married life can be summed up in a few words. For a long while she lived upon herself and distant hopes. Then, when she began to see that their narrow income put the longed-for life in Paris quite out of the question, she looked about her at the people with whom her life must be spent, and shuddered at her loneliness. There was not a single man who could inspire the madness to which women are prone when they despair of a life become stale and unprofitable in the present, and with no outlook for the future. She had nothing to look for, nothing to expect from chance, for there are lives in which chance plays no part. But when the Empire was in the full noonday of glory, and Napoleon was sending the flower of his troops to the Peninsula, her disappointed hopes revived. Natural curiosity prompted her to make an effort to see the heroes who were conquering Europe in obedience to a word from the Emperor in the order of the day; the heroes of a modern time who outdid the mythical feats of paladins of old. The cities of France, however avaricious or refractory, must perforce do honor to the Imperial Guard, and mayors and prefects went out to meet them with set speeches as if the conquerors had been crowned kings. Mme. de Bargeton went to a *ridotto* given to the town by a regiment, and fell in love with an officer of a good family, a sub-lieutenant, to whom the crafty Napoleon had given a glimpse of the baton of a Marshal of France. Love, restrained, greater and nobler than the ties that were made and unmade so easily in those days, was consecrated coldly by the hands of death. On the battlefield of Wagram a shell shattered the only record of

Mme. de Bargeton's young beauty, a portrait
worn on the heart of the Marquis of Cante-Croix.
For long afterwards she wept for the young
soldier, the colonel in his second campaign, for
the heart hot with love and glory that set a letter
from Nais above Imperial favor. The pain of
those days cast a veil of sadness over her face,
a shadow that only vanished at the terrible age
when a woman first discovers with dismay that
the best years of her life are over, and she has
had no joy of them; when she sees her roses
wither, and the longing for love is revived again
with the desire to linger yet for a little on the
last smiles of youth. Her nobler qualities dealt
so many wounds to her soul at the moment
when the cold of the provinces seized upon her.
She would have died of grief like the ermine if
by chance she had been sullied by contact with
those men whose thoughts are bent on winning
a few sous nightly at cards after a good dinner;
pride saved her from the shabby love intrigues
of the provinces. A woman so much above the
level of those about her, forced to decide
between the emptiness of the men whom she
meets and the emptiness of her own life, can
make but one choice; marriage and society
became a cloister for Anais. She lived by poetry
as the Carmelite lives by religion. All the famous
foreign books published in France for the first
time between 1815 and 1821, the great
essayists, M. de Bonald and M. de Maistre (those
two eagles of thought) – all the lighter French
literature, in short, that appeared during that

sudden outburst of first vigorous growth might bring delight into her solitary life, but not flexibility of mind or body. She stood strong and straight like some forest tree, lightning-blasted but still erect. Her dignity became a stilted manner, her social supremacy led her into affectation and sentimental over-refinements; she queened it with her foibles, after the usual fashion of those who allow their courtiers to adore them.

This was Mme. de Bargeton's past life, a dreary chronicle which must be given if Lucien's position with regard to the lady is to be comprehensible. Lucien's introduction came about oddly enough. In the previous winter a newcomer had brought some interest into Mme. de Bargeton's monotonous life. The place of controller of excise fell vacant, and M. de Barante appointed a man whose adventurous life was a sufficient passport to the house of the sovereign lady who had her share of feminine curiosity.

M. de Chatelet – he began life as plain Sixte Chatelet, but since 1806 had the wit to adopt the particle – M. du Chatelet was one of the agreeable young men who escaped conscription after conscription by keeping very close to the Imperial sun. He had begun his career as private secretary to an Imperial Highness, a post for which he possessed every qualification. Personable and of a good figure, a clever billiard-player, a passable amateur actor, he danced well, and excelled in most physical exercises; he could, moreover, sing a ballad and applaud a witticism. Supple, envious, never at a loss, there was nothing that he did not know – nothing that he really knew. He knew nothing, for instance, of music, but he could sit down to the piano and accompany, after a fashion, a woman who consented after much pressing to sing a ballad learned by heart in a month of hard practice. Incapable though he was of any feeling for poetry, he would boldly ask permission to retire for ten minutes to compose an impromptu, and return with a quatrain, flat as a pancake, wherein rhyme did duty for reason. M. du Chatelet had besides a very pretty talent for filling in the ground of the Princess' worsted work after the flowers had been begun; he held her skeins of silk with infinite grace, entertained her with dubious nothings more or less transparently veiled. He was ignorant of painting, but he could copy a landscape, sketch a head in profile, or design a costume and color it. He had, in short, all the little talents that a man could turn to such useful account in times when women exercised more influence in public life than most people imagine. Diplomacy he claimed to be his strong point; it usually is with those who have no knowledge, and are profound by reason of their emptiness; and, indeed, this kind of skill possesses one signal advantage, for it can only be displayed in the conduct of the affairs of the great, and when discretion is the quality required, a man who knows nothing can safely say nothing, and take refuge in a mysterious shake of the head; in fact; the cleverest practitioner is he who can swim with the current and keep his head well above the stream of events which he appears to control, a man's fitness for this business varying inversely as his specific gravity. But in this particular art or craft, as in all others, you shall find a thousand mediocrities for one man of genius; and in spite of Chatelet's services, ordinary and extraordinary, Her Imperial Highness could not procure a seat in the Privy Council for her private secretary; not that he would not have made a delightful Master of Requests, like many another, but the Princess was of the opinion that her secretary was better placed with her than anywhere else in the world. He was made a Baron, however, and went to Cassel as envoy-extraordinary, no empty form of words, for he cut a very extraordinary figure there − Napoleon used him as a diplomatic courier in the thick of a European crisis. Just as he had been promised the post of minister to Jerome in Westphalia, the Empire fell to pieces; and balked of his *ambassade de famille* as he called it, he went off in despair to Egypt with General de Montriveau. A strange chapter of accidents separated him from his traveling companion, and for two long years Sixte du Chatelet led a wandering life among the Arab tribes of the desert, who sold and resold their captive − his talents being not of the slightest use to the nomad tribes. At length, about the time that Montriveau reached Tangier, Chatelet found himself in the territory of the Imam of Muscat, had the luck to find an English vessel just about to set sail, and so came back to Paris a year sooner than his sometime companion. Once in Paris, his recent misfortunes, and certain connections of long standing, together with services rendered to great persons now in power, recommended him to the President of the Council, who put him in M. de Barante's department until such time as a controllership should fall vacant. So the part that M. du Chatelet once had played in the history of the Imperial Princess, his reputation for success with women, the strange story of his travels and sufferings, all awakened the interest of the ladies of Angouleme.

M. le Baron Sixte du Chatelet informed himself as to the manners and customs of the upper town, and took his cue accordingly. He appeared on the scene as a jaded man of the world, broken in health, and weary in spirit. He would raise his hand to his forehead at all seasons, as if pain never gave him a moment's respite, a habit that recalled his travels and made him interesting. He was on visiting terms with the authorities – the general in command, the prefect, the receiver-general, and the bishop but in every house he was frigid, polite, and slightly supercilious, like a man out of his proper place awaiting the favors of power. His social talents he left to conjecture, nor did they lose anything in reputation on that account; then when people began to talk about him and wish to know him, and curiosity was still lively; when he had reconnoitred the men and found them nought, and studied the women with the eyes of experience in the cathedral for several Sundays, he saw that Mme. de. Bargeton was the person with whom it would be best to be on intimate terms. Music, he thought, should open the doors of a house where strangers were never received. Surreptitiously he procured one of Miroir's Masses, learned it upon the piano; and one fine Sunday when all Angouleme went to the cathedral, he played the organ, sent those who knew no better into ecstasies over the performance, and stimulated the interest felt in him by allowing his name to slip out through the attendants. As he came out after mass, Mme. de Bargeton complimented him, regretting that she had no opportunity of playing duets with such a musician; and naturally, during an interview of her own seeking, he received the passport, which he could not have obtained if he had asked for it.

So the adroit Baron was admitted to the circle of the queen of Angouleme, and paid her marked attention. The elderly beau – he was forty-five years old – saw that all her youth lay dormant and ready to revive, saw treasures to be turned to account, and possibly a rich widow to wed, to say nothing of expectations; it would be a marriage into the family of Negrepelisse, and for him this meant a family connection with the Marquise d'Espard, and a political career in Paris.

Here was a fair tree to cultivate in spite of the ill-omened, unsightly mistletoe that grew thick upon it; he would hang his fortunes upon it, and prune it, and wait till he could gather its golden fruit.

High-born Angouleme shrieked against the introduction of a Giaour into the sanctuary, for Mme. de Bargeton's salon was a kind of holy of holies in a society that kept itself unspotted from the world. The only outsider intimate there was the bishop; the prefect was admitted twice or thrice in a year, the receiver-general was never received at all; Mme. de Bargeton would go to concerts and "at homes" at his house, but she never accepted invitations to dinner. And now, she who had declined to open her doors to the receiver-general, welcomed a mere controller of excise! Here was a novel order of precedence for snubbed authority; such a thing it had never entered their minds to conceive.

Those who by dint of mental effort can understand a kind of pettiness which, for that matter, can be found on any and every social level, will realize the awe with which the *bourgeoisie* of Angouleme regarded the Hotel de Bargeton. The inhabitant of L'Houmeau beheld the grandeur of that miniature Louvre, the glory of the Angoumoisin Hotel de Rambouillet, shining at a solar distance; and yet, within it there was gathered together all the direst intellectual poverty, all the decayed gentility from twenty leagues round about.

Political opinion expanded itself in wordy commonplaces vociferated with emphasis; the *Quotidienne* was comparatively Laodicean in its loyalty, and Louis XVIII. a Jacobin. The women, for the most part, were awkward, silly, insipid, and ill dressed; there was always something amiss that spoiled the whole; nothing in them was complete, toilette or talk, flesh or spirit. But for his designs on Mme. de Bargeton, Chatelet could not have endured the society. And yet the manners and spirit of the noble in his ruined manor-house, the knowledge of the traditions of good breeding, – these things covered a multitude of deficiencies. Nobility of feeling was far more real here than in the lofty world of Paris. You might compare these country Royalists, if the metaphor may be allowed, to old-fashioned silver plate, antiquated and tarnished, but weighty; their attachment to the House of Bourbon as the House of Bourbon did them honor. The very fixity of their political opinions was a sort of faithfulness. The distance that they set between themselves and the *bourgeoisie*, their very exclusiveness, gave them a certain elevation, and enhanced their value. Each noble represented a certain price for the townsmen, as Bambara Negroes, we are told, attach a money value to cowrie shells.

Some of the women, flattered by M. du Chatelet, discerned in him the superior qualities lacking in the men of their own sect, and the insurrection of self-love was pacified. These ladies all hoped to succeed to the Imperial Highness. Purists were of the opinion that you might see the intruder in Mme. de Bargeton's house, but not elsewhere. Du Chatelet was fain to put up with a good deal of insolence, but he held his ground by cultivating the clergy. He encouraged the queen of Angouleme in foibles bred of the soil; he brought her all the newest books; he read aloud the poetry that appeared. Together they went into ecstasies over these poets; she in all sincerity, he with suppressed yawns; but he bore with the Romantics with a patience hardly to be expected of a man of the Imperial school, who scarcely could make out what the young writers meant. Not so Mme. de Bargeton; she waxed enthusiastic over the renaissance, due to the return of the Bourbon Lilies; she loved M. de Chateaubriand for calling Victor Hugo "a sublime child." It depressed her that she could only know genius from afar, she sighed for Paris, where great men live. For these reasons M. du Chatelet thought he had done a wonderfully clever thing when he told the lady that at that moment in Angouleme there was "another sublime child," a young poet, a rising star whose glory surpassed the whole Parisian galaxy, though he knew it not. A great man of the future had been born in L'Houmeau! The headmaster of the school had shown the Baron some admirable verses. The poor and humble lad was a second Chatterton, with none of the political baseness and ferocious hatred of the great ones of earth that led his English prototype to turn pamphleteer and revile his benefactors. Mme. de Bargeton in her little circle of five or six persons, who were supposed to share her tastes for art and letters, because this one scraped a fiddle, and that splashed sheets of white paper, more or less, with sepia, and the other was president of a local agricultural society, or was gifted with a bass voice that rendered *Se fiato in corpo* like a war whoop – Mme. de Bargeton amid these grotesque figures was like a famished actor set down to a stage dinner of pasteboard. No words, therefore, can describe her joy at these tidings. She must see this poet, this angel! She raved about him, went into raptures, talked of him for whole hours together. Before two days were out the sometime diplomatic courier had negotiated (through the headmaster) for Lucien's appearance in the Hotel de Bargeton.

Poor helots of the provinces, for whom the distances between class and class are so far greater than for the Parisian (for whom, indeed, these distances visibly lessen day by day); souls so grievously oppressed by the social barriers behind which all sorts and conditions of men sit crying Raca! with mutual anathemas – you, and you alone, will fully comprehend the ferment in Lucien's heart and brain, when his awe-inspiring headmaster told him that the great gates of the Hotel de Bargeton would shortly open and turn upon their hinges at his fame! Lucien and David, walking together of an evening in the Promenade de Beaulieu, had looked up at the house with the old-fashioned gables, and wondered whether their names would ever so much as reach ears inexorably deaf to knowledge that came from a lowly origin; and now he (Lucien) was to be made welcome there!

No one except his sister was in the secret. Eve, like the thrifty housekeeper and divine magician that she was, conjured up a few louis d'or from her savings to buy thin shoes for Lucien of the best shoemaker in Angouleme, and an entirely new suit of clothes from the most renowned tailor. She made a frill for his best shirt, and washed and pleated it with her own hands. And how pleased she was to see him so dressed! How proud she felt of her brother, and what quantities of advice she gave him! Her intuition foresaw countless foolish fears. Lucien had a habit of resting his elbows on the table when he was in deep thought; he would even go so far as to draw a table nearer to lean upon it; Eve told him that he must not forget himself in those aristocratic precincts.

She went with him as far as St. Peter's Gate, and when they were almost opposite the cathedral she stopped, and watched him pass down the Rue de Beaulieu to the Promenade, where M. du Chatelet was waiting for him. And after he was out of sight, she still stood there, poor girl! in a great tremor of emotion, as though some great thing had happened to them. Lucien in Mme. de Bargeton's house! – for Eve it meant the dawn of success. The innocent creature did not suspect that where ambition begins, ingenuous feeling ends.

Externals in the Rue du Minage gave Lucien no sense of surprise. This palace, that loomed so large in his imagination, was a house built of the soft stone of the country, mellowed by time. It looked dismal enough from the street, and inside it was extremely plain; there was the usual provincial courtyard – chilly, prim, and neat; and the house itself was sober, almost convent-like, but in good repair.

Lucien went up the old staircase with the balustrade of chestnut wood (the stone steps ceased after the second floor), crossed a shabby antechamber, and came into the presence in a little wainscoted drawing-room, beyond a dimly-lit salon. The carved woodwork, in the taste of the eighteenth century, had been painted gray. There were monochrome paintings on the frieze panels, and the walls were adorned with crimson damask with a meagre border. The old-fashioned furniture shrank piteously from sight under covers of a red-and-white check pattern. On the sofa, covered with thin mattressed cushions, sat Mme. de Bargeton; the poet beheld her by the light of two wax candles on a sconce with a screen fitted to it, that stood before her on a round table with a green cloth.

The queen did not attempt to rise, but she twisted very gracefully on her seat, smiling on the poet, who was not a little fluttered by the serpentine quiverings; her manner was distinguished, he thought. For Mme. de Bargeton, she was impressed with Lucien's extreme beauty, with his diffidence, with everything about him; for her the poet already was poetry incarnate. Lucien scrutinized his hostess with discreet side glances; she disappointed none of his expectations of a great lady.

Mme. de Bargeton, following a new fashion, wore a coif of slashed black velvet, a head-dress that recalls memories of mediaeval legend to a young imagination, to amplify, as it were, the dignity of womanhood. Her red-gold hair, escaping from under her cap, hung loose; bright golden color in the light, red in the rounded shadow of the curls that only partially hid her neck. Beneath a massive white brow, clean cut and strongly outlined, shone a pair of bright gray eyes encircled by a margin of mother-of-pearl, two blue veins on each side of the nose bringing out the whiteness of that delicate setting. The Bourbon curve of the nose added to the ardent expression of an oval face; it was as if the royal temper of the House of Conde shone conspicuous in this feature. The careless cross-folds of the bodice left a white throat bare, and half revealed the outlines of a still youthful figure and shapely, well placed contours beneath.

With fingers tapering and well-kept, though somewhat too thin, Mme. de Bargeton amiably pointed to a seat by her side, M. du Chatelet ensconced himself in an easy-chair, and Lucien then became aware that there was no one else in the room.

Mme. de Bargeton's words intoxicated the young poet from L'Houmeau. For Lucien those three hours spent in her presence went by like a dream that we would fain have last forever. She was not thin, he thought; she was slender; in love with love, and loverless; and delicate in spite of her strength. Her foibles, exaggerated by her manner, took his fancy; for youth sets out with a love of hyperbole, that infirmity of noble souls. He did not so much as see that her cheeks were faded, that the patches of color on the cheek-bone were faded and hardened to a brick-red by listless days and a certain amount of ailing health. His imagination fastened at once on the glowing eyes, on the dainty curls rippling with light, on the dazzling fairness of her skin, and hovered about those bright points as the moth hovers about the candle flame. For her spirit made such appeal to his that he could no longer see the woman as she was. Her feminine exaltation had carried him away, the energy of her expressions, a little staled in truth by pretty hard and constant wear, but new to Lucien, fascinated him so much the more easily because he was determined to be pleased. He had brought none of his own verses to read, but nothing was said of them; he had purposely left them behind because he meant to return; and Mme. de Bargeton did not ask for them, because she meant that he should come back some future day to read them to her. Was not this a beginning of an understanding?

As for M. Sixte du Chatelet, he was not over well pleased with all this. He perceived rather too late in the day that he had a rival in this handsome young fellow. He went with him as far as the first flight of steps below Beaulieu to try the effect of a little diplomacy; and Lucien was not a little astonished when he heard the controller of excise pluming himself on having effected the introduction, and proceeding in this character to give him (Lucien) the benefit of his advice.

"Heaven send that Lucien might meet with better treatment than he had done," such was the matter of M. du Chatelet's discourse. "The Court was less insolent that this pack of dolts in Angouleme. You were expected to endure deadly insults; the superciliousness you had to put up with was something abominable. If this kind of folk did not alter their behavior, there would be another Revolution of '89. As for himself, if he continued to go to the house, it was because he had found Mme. de Bargeton to his taste; she was the only woman worth troubling about in Angouleme; he had been paying court to her for want of anything better to do, and now he was desperately in love with her. She would be his before very long, she loved him, everything pointed that way. The conquest of this haughty queen of the society would be his one revenge on the whole houseful of booby clodpates."

Chatelet talked of his passion in the tone of a man who would have a rival's life if he crossed his path. The elderly butterfly of the Empire came down with his whole weight on the poor poet, and tried to frighten and crush him by his self-importance. He grew taller as he gave an embellished account of his perilous wanderings; but while he impressed the poet's imagination, the lover was by no means afraid of him.

In spite of the elderly coxcomb, and regardless of his threats and airs of a *bourgeois* bravo, Lucien went back again and again to the house – not too often at first, as became a man of L'Houmeau; but before very long he grew accustomed to the vast condescension, as it had seemed to him at the outset, and came more and more frequently. The druggist's son was a completely insignificant being. If any of the *noblesse*, men or women, calling upon Nais, found Lucien in the room, they met him with the overwhelming graciousness that well-bred people use towards their inferiors. Lucien thought them very kind for a time, and later found out the real reason for their specious amiability. It was not long before he detected a patronizing tone that stirred his gall and confirmed him in his bitter Republicanism, a phase of opinion through which many a would-be patrician passes by way of prelude to his introduction to polite society.

But was there anything that he would not have endured for Nais? – for so he heard her named by the clan. Like Spanish grandees and the old Austrian nobility at Vienna, these folk, men and women alike, called each other by their Christian names, a final shade of distinction in the inmost ring of Angoumoisin aristocracy.

Lucien loved Nais as a young man loves the first woman who flatters him, for Nais prophesied great things and boundless fame for Lucien. She used all her skill to secure her hold upon her poet; not merely did she exalt him beyond measure, but she represented him to himself as a child without fortune whom she meant to start in life; she treated him like a child, to keep him near her; she made him her reader, her secretary, and cared more for him than she would have thought possible after the dreadful calamity that had befallen her.

She was very cruel to herself in those days, telling herself that it would be folly to love a young man of twenty, so far apart from her socially in the first place; and her behavior to him was a bewildering mixture of familiarity and capricious fits of pride arising from her fears and scruples. She was sometimes a lofty patroness, sometimes she was tender and flattered him. At first, while he was overawed by her rank, Lucien experienced the extremes of dread, hope, and despair, the torture of a first love, that is beaten deep into the heart with the hammer strokes of alternate bliss and anguish. For two months Mme. de Bargeton was for him a benefactress who would take a mother's interest in him; but confidences came next. Mme. de Bargeton began to address her poet as "dear Lucien," and then as "dear," without more ado. The poet grew bolder, and addressed the great lady as Nais, and there followed a flash of anger that captivates a boy; she reproached him for calling her by a name in everybody's mouth. The haughty and high-born Negrepelisse offered the fair angel youth that one of her appellations which was unsoiled by use; for him she would be "Louise." Lucien was in the third heaven.

One evening when Lucien came in, he found Mme. de Bargeton looking at a portrait, which she promptly put away. He wished to see it, and to quiet the despair of a first fit of jealousy Louise showed him Cante-Croix's picture, and told with tears the piteous story of a love so stainless, so cruelly cut short. Was she experimenting with herself? Was she trying a first unfaithfulness to the memory of the dead? Or had she taken it into her head to raise up a rival to Lucien in the portrait? Lucien was too much of a boy to analyze his lady-love; he gave way to unfeigned despair when she opened the campaign by entrenching herself behind the more or less skilfully devised scruples which women raise to have them battered down. When a woman begins to talk about her duty, regard for appearances or religion, the objections she raises are so many redoubts which she loves to have carried by storm. But on the guileless Lucien these coquetries were thrown away; he would have advanced of his own accord.

"I shall not die for you, I will live for you," he cried audaciously one evening; he meant to have no more of M. de Cante-Croix, and gave Louise a glance which told plainly that a crisis was at hand.

Startled at the progress of this new love in herself and her poet, Louise demanded some verses promised for the first page of her album, looking for a pretext for a quarrel in his tardiness. But what became of her when she read the following stanzas, which, naturally, she considered finer than the finest work of Canalis, the poet of the aristocracy?–

> The magic brush, light flying flights of song–
> To these, but not to these alone, belong
> My pages fair;

Often to me, my mistress' pencil steals
To tell the secret gladness that she feels,
The hidden care.

And when her fingers, slowlier at the last,
Of a rich Future, now become the Past,
Seek count of me,
Oh Love, when swift, thick-coming
memories rise,
I pray of Thee.
May they bring visions fair as cloudless
skies
Of happy voyage o'er a summer sea!

"Was it really I who inspired those lines?" she
asked.

The doubt suggested by coquetry to a woman
who amused herself by playing with fire
brought tears to Lucien's eyes; but her first
kiss upon his forehead calmed the storm. Decidedly Lucien was a great man, and she
meant to form him; she thought of teaching
him Italian and German and perfecting his
manners. That would be pretext sufficient for
having him constantly with her under the very
eyes of her tiresome courtiers. What an interest in her life! She took up music again for
her poet's sake, and revealed the world of
sound to him, playing grand fragments of
Beethoven till she sent him into ecstasy; and,
happy in his delight, turned to the half-
swooning poet.

"Is not such happiness as this enough?" she asked hypocritically; and poor Lucien was stupid enough to answer, "Yes."

In the previous week things had reached such a point, that Louise had judged it expedient to ask Lucien to dine with M. de Bargeton as a third. But in spite of this precaution, the whole town knew the state of affairs; and so extraordinary did it appear, that no one would believe the truth. The outcry was terrific. Some were of the opinion that society was on the eve of cataclysm. "See what comes of Liberal doctrines!" cried others.

Then it was that the jealous du Chatelet discovered that Madame Charlotte, the monthly nurse, was no other than Mme. Chardon, "the mother of the Chateaubriand of L'Houmeau," as he put it. The remark passed muster as a joke. Mme. de Chandour was the first to hurry to Mme. de Bargeton.

"Nais, dear," she said, "do you know what everybody is talking about in Angouleme? This little rhymster's mother is the Madame Charlotte who nursed my sister-in-law through her confinement two months ago."

"What is there extraordinary in that, my dear?" asked Mme. de Bargeton with her most regal air. "She is a druggist's widow, is she not? A poor fate for a Rubempre. Suppose that you and

I had not a penny in the world, what should either of us do for a living? How would you support your children?"

Mme. de Bargeton's presence of mind put an end to the jeremiads of the *noblesse*. Great natures are prone to make a virtue of misfortune; and there is something irresistibly attractive about well-doing when persisted in through evil report; innocence has the piquancy of the forbidden.

Mme. de Bargeton's rooms were crowded that evening with friends who came to remonstrate with her. She brought her most caustic wit into play. She said that as noble families could not produce a Moliere, a Racine, a Rousseau, a Voltaire, a Massillon, a Beaumarchais, or a Diderot, people must make up their minds to it, and accept the fact that great men had upholsterers and clockmakers and cutlers for their fathers. She said that genius was always noble. She railed at boorish squires for understanding their real interests so imperfectly. In short, she talked a good deal of nonsense, which would have let the light into heads less dense, but left her audience agape at her eccentricity. And in these ways she conjured away the storm with her heavy artillery.

When Lucien, obedient to her request, appeared for the first time in the faded great drawing-room, where the whist-tables were set out, she welcomed him graciously, and brought him forward, like a queen who means to be obeyed. She addressed the controller of excise as "M. Chatelet," and left that gentleman thunderstruck by the discovery that she knew about the illegal superfetation of the particle. Lucien was forced upon her circle, and was received as a poisonous element, which every person in it vowed to expel with the antidote of insolence.

Nais had won a victory, but she had lost her supremacy of empire. There was a rumor of insurrection. Amelie, otherwise Mme. de Chandour, harkening to "M. Chatelet's" counsels, determined to erect a rival altar by receiving on Wednesdays. Now Mme. de Bargeton's salon was open every evening; and those who frequented it were so wedded to their ways, so accustomed to meet about the same tables, to play the familiar game of backgammon, to see the same faces and the same candle sconces night after night; and afterwards to cloak and shawl, and put on overshoes and hats in the old corridor, that they were quite as much attached to the steps of the staircase as to the mistress of the house.

"All resigned themselves to endure the songster (chardonneret) of the sacred grove," said Alexandre de Brebian, which was witticism number two. Finally, the president of the agricultural society put an end to the sedition by remarking judicially that "before the Revolution the greatest nobles admitted men like Dulcos and Grimm and Crebillon to their society – men who were nobodies, like this little poet of L'Houmeau; but one thing they never did, they never received tax-collectors, and, after all, Chatelet is only a tax-collector."

Du Chatelet suffered for Chardon. Every one turned the cold shoulder upon him; and Chatelet was conscious that he was attacked. When Mme. de Bargeton called him "M. Chatelet," he swore to himself that he would possess her; and now he entered into the views of the mistress of the house, came to the support of the young poet, and declared himself Lucien's friend. The great diplomatist, overlooked by the shortsighted Emperor, made much of Lucien, and declared himself his friend! To launch the poet into society, he gave a dinner, and asked all the authorities to meet him – the prefect, the receiver-general, the colonel in command of the garrison, the head of the Naval School, the president of the Court, and so forth. The poet, poor fellow, was feted so magnificently, and so belauded, that anybody but a young man of two-and-twenty would have shrewdly suspected a hoax. After dinner, Chatelet drew his rival on to recite *The Dying Sardanapalus*, the masterpiece of the hour; and the headmaster of the school, a man of a phlegmatic temperament, applauded with both hands, and vowed that Jean-Baptiste Rousseau had done nothing finer.

Sixte, Baron du Chatelet, thought in his heart that this slip of a rhymster would wither incontinently in a hothouse of adulation; perhaps he hoped that when the poet's head was turned with brilliant dreams, he would indulge in some impertinence that would promptly consign him to the obscurity from which he had emerged. Pending the decease of genius, Chatelet appeared to offer up his hopes as a sacrifice at Mme. de Bargeton's feet; but with the ingenuity of a rake, he kept his own plan in abeyance, watching the lovers' movements with keenly critical eyes, and waiting for the opportunity of ruining Lucien.

From this time forward, vague rumors reported the existence of a great man in Angoumois. Mme. de Bargeton was praised on all sides for the interest which she took in this young eagle. No sooner was her conduct approved than she tried to win a general sanction. She announced a soiree, with ices, tea, and cakes, a great innovation in a city where tea, as yet, was sold only by druggists as a remedy for indigestion. The flower of Angoumoisin aristocracy was summoned to hear Lucien read his great work. Louise had hidden all the difficulties from her friend, but she let fall a few words touching the social cabal formed against him; she would not have him ignorant of the perils besetting his career as a man of genius, nor of the obstacles insurmountable to weaklings. She drew a lesson from the recent victory. Her white hands pointed him to glory that lay beyond a prolonged martyrdom; she spoke of stakes and flaming pyres; she spread the adjectives thickly on her finest tartines, and decorated them with a variety of her most pompous epithets. It was an infringement of the copyright of the passages of declamation that disfigure *Corinne*; but Louise grew so much the greater in her own eyes as she talke, that she loved the Benjamin who inspired her eloquence the more for it. She counseled him to take a bold step and renounce his patronymic for the noble name of Rubempre; he need not mind the little tittle-tattle over a change which the King, for that matter, would authorize. Mme. de Bargeton undertook to procure this favor; she was related to the Marquise d'Espard, who was a Blamont-Chauvry before her marriage, and a *persona grata* at Court. The words "King," "Marquise d'Espard," and "the Court" dazzled Lucien like a blaze of fireworks, and the necessity of the baptism was plain to him.

"Dear child," said Louise, with tender mockery in her tones, "the sooner it is done, the sooner it will be sanctioned."

She went through social strata and showed the poet that this step would raise him many rungs higher in the ladder. Seizing the moment, she persuaded Lucien to forswear the chimerical notions of '89 as to equality; she roused a thirst for social distinction allayed by David's cool commonsense; she pointed out fashionable society as the goal and the only stage for such a talent as his. The rabid Liberal became a Monarchist in *petto*; Lucien set his teeth in the apple of desire of rank, luxury, and fame. He swore to win a crown to lay at his lady's feet, even if there should be blood-stains on the bays. He would conquer at any cost, *quibuscumque viis*. To prove his courage, he told her of his present way of life; Louise had known nothing of its hardships, for there is an indefinable pudency inseparable from strong feeling in youth, a delicacy which shrinks from a display of great qualities; and a young man loves to have the real quality of his nature discerned through the incognito. He described that life, the shackles of poverty borne with pride, his days of work for David, his nights of study. His young ardor recalled memories of the colonel of six-and-twenty; Mme. de Bargeton's eyes grew soft; and Lucien, seeing this weakness in his awe-inspiring mistress, seized a hand that she had abandoned to him, and kissed it with the frenzy of a lover and a poet in his youth. Louise even allowed him to set his eager, quivering lips upon her forehead.

"Oh, child! child! if any one should see us, I should look very ridiculous," she said, shaking off the ecstatic torpor.

In the course of that evening, Mme. de Bargeton's wit made havoc of Lucien's prejudices, as she styled them. Men of genius, according to her doctrine, had neither brothers nor sisters nor father nor mother; the great tasks laid upon them required that they should sacrifice everything that they might grow to their full stature. Perhaps their families might suffer at first from the all-absorbing exactions of a giant brain, but at a later day they were repaid a hundredfold for self-denial of every kind during the early struggles of the kingly intellect with adverse fate; they shared the spoils of victory. Genius was answerable to no man. Genius alone could judge of the means used to an end which no one else could know. It was the duty of a man of genius, therefore, to set himself above law; it was his mission to reconstruct law; the man who is master of his age may take all that he needs, run any risks, for all is his. She quoted instances. Bernard Palissy, Louis XI., Fox, Napoleon, Christopher Columbus, and Julius Caesar, – all these world-famous gamblers had begun life hampered with debt, or as poor men; all of them had been misunderstood, taken for madmen, reviled for bad sons, bad brothers, bad fathers; and yet in after life each one had come to be the pride of his family, of his country, of the civilized world.

Her arguments fell upon fertile soil in the worst of Lucien's nature, and spread corruption in his heart; for him, when his desires were hot, all means were admissible. But – failure is high treason against society; and when the fallen

conqueror has run amuck through *bourgeois*
virtues, and pulled down the pillars of society,
small wonder that society, finding Marius seated
among the ruins, should drive him forth in ab-
horrence. All unconsciously Lucien stood with
the palm of genius on the one hand and a
shameful ending in the hulks upon the other;
and, on high upon the Sinai of the prophets,
beheld no Dead Sea covering the cities of the
plain – the hideous winding-sheet of Gomorrah.

So well did Louise loosen the swaddling-bands
of provincial life that confined the heart and
brain of her poet that the said poet determined
to try an experiment upon her. He wished to
feel certain that this proud conquest was his
without laying himself open to the mortification
of a rebuff. The forthcoming soiree gave him
his opportunity. Ambition blended with his love.
He loved, and he meant to rise, a double desire
not unnatural in young men with a heart to
satisfy and the battle of life to fight. Society,
summoning all her children to one banquet,
arouses ambition in the very morning of life.
Youth is robbed of its charm, and generous
thoughts are corrupted by mercenary scheming.
The idealist would fain have it otherwise, but
intrusive fact too often gives the lie to the fiction which we should like to believe, making
it impossible to paint the young man of the
nineteenth century other than he is. Lucien
imagined that his scheming was entirely
prompted by good feeling, and persuaded him-

self that it was done solely for his friend David's sake.

He wrote a long letter to his Louise; he felt bolder, pen in hand, than face to face. In a dozen sheets, copied out three several times, he told her of his father's genius and blighted hopes and of his grinding poverty. He described his beloved sister as an angel, and David as another Cuvier, a great man of the future, and a father, friend, and brother to him in the present. He should feel himself unworthy of his Louise's love (his proudest distinction) if he did not ask her to do for David all that she had done for him. He would give up everything rather than desert David Sechard; David must witness his success. It was one of those wild letters in which a young man points a pistol at a refusal, letters full of boyish casuistry and the incoherent reasoning of an idealist; a delicious tissue of words embroidered here and there by the naive utterances that women love so well – unconscious revelations of the writer's heart.

Lucien left the letter with the housemaid, went to the office, and spent the day in reading proofs, superintending the execution of orders, and looking after the affairs of the printing-house. He said not a word to David. While youth bears a child's heart, it is capable of sublime reticence. Perhaps, too, Lucien began to dread the Phocion's axe which David could wield when he chose, perhaps he was afraid to meet those clear-sighted eyes that read the depths of his soul. But when he read Chenier's poems with David, his secret rose from his heart to his lips at the sting of a reproach that he felt as the patient feels the probing of a wound.

And now try to understand the thoughts that troubled Lucien's mind as he went down from Angouleme. Was the great lady angry with him? Would she receive David? Had he, Lucien, in his ambition, flung himself headlong back into the depths of L'Houmeau? Before he set that kiss on Louise's forehead, he had had time to measure the distance between a queen and her favorite, so far had he come in five months, and he did not tell himself that David could cross over the same ground in a moment. Yet he did not know how completely the lower orders were excluded from this upper world; he did not so much as suspect that a second experiment of this kind meant ruin for Mme. de Bargeton. Once accused and fairly convicted of a liking for *canaille*, Louise would be driven from the place, her caste would shun her as men shunned a leper in the Middle Ages. Nais might have broken the moral law, and her whole circle, the clergy and the flower of the aristocracy, would have defended her against the world through thick and then; but a breach of another law, the offence of admitting all sorts of people to her house – this was sin without remission. The sins of those in power are always overlooked – once let them abdicate, and they shall pay the penalty. And what was it but abdication to receive David?

But if Lucien did not see these aspects of the question, his aristocratic instinct discerned plenty of difficulties of another kind, and he took alarm. A fine manner is not the invariable outcome of noble feeling; and while no man at court had a nobler air than Racine, Corneille looked very much like a cattle-dealer, and Descartes might have been taken for an honest Dutch merchant; and visitors to La Brede, meeting Montesquieu in a cotton nightcap, carrying a rake over his shoulder, mistook him for a gardener. A knowledge of the world, when it is not sucked in with mother's milk and part of the inheritance of descent, is only acquired by education, supplemented by certain gifts of chance – a graceful figure, distinction of feature, a certain ring in the voice. All these, so important trifles, David lacked, while Nature had bestowed them upon his friend. Of gentle blood on the mother's side, Lucien was a Frank, even down to the high-arched instep. David had inherited the physique of his father the pressman and the flat foot of the Gael. Lucien could hear the shower of jokes at David's expense; he could see Mme. de Bargeton's repressed smile; and at length, without being exactly ashamed of his brother, he made up his mind to disregard his first impulse and to think twice before yielding to it in future.

So, after the hour of poetry and self-sacrifice, after the reading of verse that opened out before the friends the fields of literature in the light of a newly-risen sun, the hour of worldly wisdom and of scheming struck for Lucien.

Down once more in L'Houmeau he wished that he had not written that letter; he wished he could have it back again; for down the vista of the future he caught a glimpse of the inexorable laws of the world. He guessed that nothing succeeds like success, and it cost him something to step down from the first rung of the scaling ladder by which he meant to reach and storm the heights above. Pictures of his quiet and simple life rose before him, pictures fair with the brightest colors of blossoming love. There was David; what a genius David had – David who had helped him so generously, and would die for him at need; he thought of his mother, of how great a lady she was in her lowly lot, and how she thought that he was as good as he was clever; then of his sister so gracious in submission to her fate, of his own innocent childhood and conscience as yet unstained, of budding hopes undespoiled by rough winds, and at these thoughts the past broke into flowers once more for his memory.

Then he told himself that it was a far finer thing to hew his own way through serried hostile mobs of aristocrats or philistines by repeated successful strokes, than to reach the goal through a woman's favor. Sooner or later his genius should shine out; it had been so with the others, his predecessors; they had tamed society. Women would love him when that day came! The example of Napoleon, which, unluckily for this nineteenth century of ours, has filled a great many ordinary persons with aspirations after extraordinary destinies, – the example of Napoleon occurred to Lucien's mind. He flung his schemes to the winds and blamed himself for thinking of them. For Lucien was so made that he went from evil to good, or from good to evil, with the same facility.

Lucien had none of the scholar's love for his retreat; for the past month indeed he had felt something like shame at the sight of the shop front, where you could read–

POSTEL (LATE CHARDON), HARMACEUTICAL CHEMIST,

in yellow letters on a green ground. It was an offence to him that his father's name should be thus posted up in a place where every carriage passed.

Every evening, when he closed the ugly iron gate and went up to Beaulieu to give his arm to Mme. de Bargeton among the dandies of the upper town, he chafed beyond all reason at the disparity between his lodging and his fortune.

"I love Mme. de Bargeton; perhaps in a few days she will be mine, yet here I live in this rat-hole!" he said to himself this evening, as he went down the narrow passage into the little yard behind the shop. This evening bundles of boiled herbs were spread out along the wall, the apprentice was scouring a caldron, and M. Postel himself, girded about with his laboratory apron, was standing with a retort in his hand, inspecting some chemical product while keeping an eye upon the shop door, or if the eye happened to be engaged, he had at any rate an ear for the bell.

A strong scent of camomile and peppermint pervaded the yard and the poor little dwelling at the side, which you reached by a short ladder, with a rope on either side by way of hand-rail. Lucien's room was an attic just under the roof.

"Good-day, sonny," said M. Postel, that typical, provincial tradesman. "Are you pretty middling? I have just been experimenting on treacle, but it would take a man like your father to find what I am looking for. Ah! he was a famous chemist, he was! If I had only known his gout specific, you and I should be rolling along in our carriage this day."

The little druggist, whose head was as thick as his heart was kind, never let a week pass without some allusion to Chardon senior's unlucky secretiveness as to that discovery, words that Lucien felt like a stab.

"It is a great pity," Lucien answered curtly. He was beginning to think his father's apprentice prodigiously vulgar, though he had blessed the man for his kindness, for honest Postel had helped his master's widow and children more than once.

"Why, what is the matter with you?" M. Postel inquired, putting down his test tube on the laboratory table.

"Is there a letter for me?"

"Yes, a letter that smells like balm! it is lying on the corner near my desk."

Mme. de Bargeton's letter lying among the physic bottles in a druggist's shop! Lucien sprang in to rescue it.

"Be quick, Lucien! your dinner has been waiting an hour for you, it will be cold!" a sweet voice called gently through a half-opened window; but Lucien did not hear.

"That brother of yours has gone crazy, mademoiselle," said Postel, lifting his face.

The old bachelor looked rather like a miniature brandy cask, embellished by a painter's fancy, with a fat, ruddy countenance much pitted with the smallpox; at the sight of Eve his face took a ceremonious and amiable expression, which said plainly that he had thoughts of espousing the daughter of his predecessor, but could not put an end to the strife between love and interest in his heart. He often said to Lucien, with a smile, "Your sister is uncommonly pretty, and you are not so bad looking neither! Your father did everything well."

Eve was tall, dark-haired, dark of complexion, and blue-eyed; but notwithstanding these signs of virile character, she was gentle, tender-hearted, and devoted to those she loved. Her frank innocence, her simplicity, her quiet acceptance of a hard-working life, her character – for her life was above reproach – could not fail to win David Sechard's heart. So, since the first time that these two had met, a repressed and single-hearted love had grown up between them in the German fashion, quietly, with no fervid protestations. In their secret souls they thought of each other as if there were a bar between that kept them apart; as if the thought were an offence against some jealous husband; and hid their feelings from Lucien as though their love in some way did him a wrong. David, moreover, had no confidence in himself, and could not believe that Eve could care for him; Eve was a penniless girl, and therefore shy. A real work-girl would have been bolder; but Eve, gently bred, and fallen into poverty, resigned herself to her dreary lot. Diffident as she seemed, she was in reality proud, and would not make a single advance towards the son of a father said to be rich. People who knew the value of a growing property, said that the vineyard at Marsac was worth more than eighty thousand francs, to say nothing of the traditional bits of land which old Sechard used to buy as they came into the market, for old Sechard had savings – he was lucky with his vintages, and a clever salesman. Perhaps David was the only man in Angouleme who knew nothing of his father's wealth. In David's eyes Marsac was a hovel bought in 1810 for fifteen or sixteen thousand francs, a place that he saw once a year at vintage time when his father walked him up and down among the vines and boasted of an output of wine which the young printer never saw, and he cared nothing about it.

David was a student leading a solitary life; and the love that gained even greater force in solitude, as he dwelt upon the difficulties in the way, was timid, and looked for encouragement; for David stood more in awe of Eve than a simple clerk of some high-born lady. He was awkward and ill at ease in the presence of his idol, and as eager to hurry away as he had been to come. He repressed his passion, and was silent. Often of an evening, on some pretext of consulting Lucien, he would leave the Place du Murier and go down through the Palet Gate as far as L'Houmeau, but at the sight of the green iron railings his heart failed. Perhaps he had come too late, Eve might think him a nuisance; she would be in bed by this time no doubt; and so he turned back. But though his great love had only appeared in trifles, Eve read it clearly; she was proud, without a touch of vanity in her pride, of the deep reverence in David's looks and words and manner towards her, but it was the young printer's enthusiastic belief in Lucien that drew her to him most of all. He had divined the way to win Eve. The mute delights of this love of theirs differed from the transports of stormy passion, as wildflowers in the fields from the brilliant flowers in garden beds. Interchange of glances, delicate and sweet as blue water-flowers on the surface of the stream; a look in either face, vanishing as swiftly as the scent of briar-rose; melancholy, tender as the velvet of moss – these were the blossoms of two rare natures, springing up out of a rich and fruitful soil on foundations of rock. Many a time Eve had seen revelations of the strength that lay below the appearance of weakness, and made such full allowance for all that David left undone, that the slightest word now might bring about a closer union of soul and soul.

Eve opened the door, and Lucien sat down without a word at the little table on an X-shaped trestle. There was no tablecloth; the poor little household boasted but three silver spoons and forks, and Eve had laid them all for the dearly loved brother.

"What have you there?" she asked, when she had set a dish on the table, and put the extinguisher on the portable stove, where it had been kept hot for him.

Lucien did not answer. Eve took up a little plate, daintily garnished with vine-leaves, and set it on the table with a jug full of cream.

"There, Lucien, I have had strawberries for you."

But Lucien was so absorbed in his letter that he did not hear a word. Eve came to sit beside him without a murmur; for in a sister's love for a brother it is an element of great pleasure to be treated without ceremony.

"Oh! what is it?" she cried as she saw tears shining in her brother's eyes.

"Nothing, nothing, Eve," he said, and putting his arm about her waist, he drew her towards him and kissed her forehead, her hair, her throat, with warmth that surprised her.

"You are keeping something from me."

"Well, then – she loves me."

"I knew very well that you kissed me for somebody else," the poor sister pouted, flushing red.

"We shall all be happy," cried Lucien, swallowing great spoonfuls of soup.

"*We*?" echoed Eve. The same presentiment that had crossed David's mind prompted her to add, "You will not care so much about us now."

"How can you think that, if you know me?"

Eve put out her hand and grasped his tightly; then she carried off the empty plate and the brown earthen soup-tureen, and brought the dish that she had made for him. But instead of eating his dinner, Lucien read his letter over again; and Eve, discreet maiden, did not ask another question, respecting her brother's silence. If he wished to tell her about it, she could wait; if he did not, how could she ask him to tell her? She waited. Here is the letter:-

"MY FRIEND, – Why should I refuse to your brother in science the help that I have lent you? All merits have equal rights in my eyes; but you do not know the prejudices of those among whom I live. We shall never make an aristocracy of ignorance understand that intellect ennobles. If I have not sufficient influence to compel them to accept M. David Sechard, I am quite willing to sacrifice the worthless creatures to you. It would be a perfect hecatomb in the antique manner. But, dear friend, you would not, of course, ask me to leave them all in exchange for the society of a person whose character and manner might not please me. I know from your flatteries how easily friendship can be blinded. Will you think the worse of me if I attach a condition to my consent? In the interests of your future I should like to see your friend, and know and decide for myself whether you are not mistaken. What is this but the mother's anxious care of my dear poet, which I am in duty bound to take?

"LOUISE DE NEGREPELISSE."

Lucien had no suspicion of the art with which polite society puts forward a "Yes" on the way to a "No," and a "No" that leads to a "Yes." He took this note for a victory. David should go to Mme. de Bargeton's house! David would shine there in all the majesty of his genius! He raised his head so proudly in the intoxication of a victory which increased his belief in himself and his ascendency over others, his face was so radiant with the brightness of many hopes, that his sister could not help telling him that he looked handsome.

"If that woman has any sense, she must love you! And if so, to-night she will be vexed, for all the ladies will try all sorts of coquetries on you. How handsome you will look when you read your *Saint John in Patmos*! If only I were a mouse, and could just slip in and see it! Come, I have put your clothes out in mother's room."

The mother's room bore witness to self-respecting poverty. There were white curtains to the walnut wood bedstead, and a strip of cheap green carpet at the foot. A chest of drawers with a wooden top, a looking-glass, and a few walnut wood chairs completed the furniture. The clock on the chimney-piece told of the old vanished days of prosperity. White curtains hung in the windows, a gray flowered paper covered the walls, and the tiled floor, colored and waxed by Eve herself, shone with cleanliness. On the little round table in the middle of the room stood a red tray with a pattern of gilt roses, and three cups and a sugar-basin of Limoges porcelain. Eve slept in the little adjoining closet, where there was just room for a narrow bed, an old-fashioned low chair, and a work-table by the window; there was about as much space as there is in a ship's cabin, and the door always stood open for the sake of air. But if all these things spoke of great poverty, the atmosphere was sedate and studious; and for those who knew the mother and children, there was something touchingly appropriate in their surroundings.

Lucien was tying his cravat when David's step sounded outside in the little yard, and in another moment the young printer appeared.

From his manner and looks he seemed to have come down in a hurry.

"Well, David!" cried the ambitious poet, "we have gained the day! She loves me! You shall come too."

"No," David said with some confusion, "I came down to thank you for this proof of friendship, but I have been thinking things over seriously. My own life is cut out for me, Lucien. I am David Sechard, printer to His Majesty in Angouleme, with my name at the bottom of the bills posted on every wall. For people of that class, I am an artisan, or I am in business, if you like it better, but I am a craftsman who lives over a shop in the Rue de Beaulieu at the corner of the Place du Murier. I have not the wealth of a Keller just yet, nor the name of a Desplein, two sorts of power that the nobles still try to ignore, and – I am so far agreed with them – this power is nothing without a knowledge of the world and the manners of a gentleman. How am I to prove my claim to this sudden elevation? I should only make myself a laughing-stock for nobles and *bourgeoisie* to boot. As for you, your position is different. A foreman is not committed to anything. You are busy gaining knowledge that will be indispensable by and by; you can explain your present work by your future. And, in any case, you can leave your place tomorrow and begin something else; you might study law or diplomacy, or go into civil service. Nobody had docketed and pigeon-holed *you*, in fact. Take advantage of your social maiden fame to walk alone and grasp honors. Enjoy all pleasures gladly, even frivolous pleasures. I wish you luck, Lucien; I shall enjoy your success; you will be like a second self for me. Yes, in my own thoughts I shall live your life. You shall have the holiday life, in the glare of the world and among the swift working springs of intrigue. I will lead the work-a-day life, the tradesman's life of sober toil, and the patient labor of scientific research.

"You shall be our aristocracy," he went on, looking at Eve as he spoke. "If you totter, you shall have my arm to steady you. If you have reason to complain of the treachery of others, you will find a refuge in our hearts, the love there will never change. And influence and favor and the goodwill of others might fail us if we were two; we should stand in each other's way; go forward, you can tow me after you if it comes to that. So far from envying you, I will dedicate my life to yours. The thing that you have just done for me, when you risked the loss of your benefactress, your love it may be, rather than forsake or disown me, that little thing, so great as it was – ah, well, Lucien, that in itself would bind me to you forever if we were not brothers already. Have no remorse, no concern over seeming to take the larger share. This one-sided bargain is exactly to my taste. And, after all, suppose that you should give me a pang now and again, who knows that I shall not still be your debtor all my life long?"

He looked timidly towards Eve as he spoke; her eyes were full of tears, she saw all that lay below the surface.

"In fact," he went on, turning to Lucien, who stood amazed at this, "you are well made, you have a graceful figure, you wear your clothes with an air, you look like a gentleman in that blue coat of yours with the yellow buttons and the plain nankeen trousers; now I should look like a workingman among those people, I should be awkward and out of my element, I should say foolish things, or say nothing at all; but as for you, you can overcome any prejudice as to names by taking your mother's; you can call yourself Lucien de Rubempre; I am and always shall be David Sechard. In this society that you frequent, everything tells for you, everything would tell against me. You were born to shine in it. Women will worship that angel face of yours; won't they, Eve?"

Lucien sprang up and flung his arms about David. David's humility had made short work of many doubts and plenty of difficulties. Was it possible not to feel twice tenderly towards this friend, who by the way of friendship had come to think the very thoughts that he, Lucien, had reached through ambition? The aspirant for love and honors felt that the way had been made smooth for him; the young man and the comrade felt all his heart go out towards his friend.

It was one of those moments that come very seldom in our lives, when all the forces in us are sweetly strung, and every chord vibrating gives out full resonance.

And yet, this goodness of a noble nature increased Lucien's human tendency to take himself as the centre of things. Do not all of us say more or less, "*L'Etat, c'est moi!*" with Louis Quatorze? Lucien's mother and sister had concentrated all their tenderness on him, David was his devoted friend; he was accustomed to see the three making every effort for him in secret, and consequently he had all the faults of a spoiled eldest son. The noble is eaten up with the egoism which their unselfishness was fostering in Lucien; and Mme. de Bargeton was doing her best to develop the same fault by inciting him to forget all that he owed to his sister, and mother, and David. He was far from doing so as yet; but was there not ground for the fear that as his sphere of ambition widened, his whole thought perforce would be how he might maintain himself in it?

When emotion had subsided, David had a suggestion to make. He thought that Lucien's poem, *Saint John in Patmos*, was possibly too biblical to be read before an audience but little familiar with apocalyptic poetry. Lucien, making his first appearance before the most exacting public in the Charente, seemed to be nervous. David advised him to take Andre de Chenier and substitute certain pleasure for a dubious delight. Lucien was a perfect reader, the listeners would enjoy listening to him, and his modesty would doubtless serve him well. Like most young people, the pair were endowing the rest of the world with their own intelligence and virtues; for if youth that has not yet gone astray is pitiless for the sins of others, it is ready, on the other hand, to put a magnificent faith in them. It is only, in fact, after a good deal of experience of life that we recognize the truth of Raphael's great saying – "To comprehend is to equal."

The power of appreciating poetry is rare, generally speaking, in France; *esprit* soon dries up the source of the sacred tears of ecstasy; nobody cares to be at the trouble of deciphering the sublime, of plumbing the depths to discover the infinite. Lucien was about to have his first experience of the ignorance and indifference of worldlings. He went round by way of the printing office for David's volume of poetry.

The two lovers were left alone, and David had never felt more embarrassed in his life. Countless terrors seized upon him; he half wished, half feared that Eve would praise him; he longed to run away, for even modesty is not exempt from coquetry. David was afraid to utter a word that might seem to beg for thanks; everything that he could think of put him in some false position, so he held his tongue and looked guilty. Eve, guessing the agony of modesty, was enjoying the pause; but when David twisted his hat as if he meant to go, she looked at him and smiled.

"Monsieur David," she said, "if you are not going to pass the evening at Mme. de Bargeton's, we can spend the time together. It is fine; shall we take a walk along the Charente? We will have a talk about Lucien."

David longed to fling himself at the feet of this delicious girl. Eve had rewarded him beyond his hopes by that tone in her voice; the kindness of her accent had solved the difficulties of the position, her suggestion was something better than praise; it was the first grace given by love.

"But give me time to dress!" she said, as David made as if to go at once.

David went out; he who all his life long had not known one tune from another, was humming to himself; honest Postel hearing him with surprise, conceived a vehement suspicion of Eve's feelings towards the printer.

The most trifling things that happened that evening made a great impression on Lucien, and his character was peculiarly susceptible to first impressions. Like all inexperienced lovers he arrived so early that Louise was not in the drawing-room; but M. de Bargeton was there, alone. Lucien had already begun to serve his apprenticeship in the practice of the small deceits with which the lover of a married woman pays for his happiness – deceits through which, moreover, she learns the extent of her power; but so far Lucien had not met the lady's husband face to face.

M. de Bargeton's intellect was of the limited kind, exactly poised on the border line between harmless vacancy, with some glimmerings of sense, and the excessive stupidity that can neither take in nor give out any idea. He was thoroughly impressed with the idea of doing his duty in society; and, doing his utmost to be agreeable, had adopted the smile of an opera dancer as his sole method of expression. Satisfied, he smiled; dissatisfied, he smiled again. He smiled at good news and evil tidings; with slight modifications the smile did duty on all occasions. If he was positively obliged to express his personal approval, a complacent laugh reinforced the smile; but he never vouchsafed a word until driven to the last extremity. A *tete-a-tete* put him in the one embarrassment of his vegetative existence, for then he was obliged to look for something to say in the vast blank of his vacant interior. He usually got out of the difficulty by a return to the artless ways of childhood; he thought aloud, took you into his confidence concerning the smallest details of his existence, his physical wants, the small sensations which did duty for ideas with him. He never talked about the weather, nor did he indulge in the ordinary commonplaces of conversation – the way of escape provided for weak intellects; he plunged you into the most intimate and personal topics.

"I took veal this morning to please Mme. de Bargeton, who is very fond of veal, and my stomach has been very uneasy since," he would tell you. "I knew how it would be; it never suits me. How do you explain it?" Or, very likely–

"I am just about to ring for a glass of *eau sucree*; will you have some at the same time?"

Or, "I am going to take a ride to-morrow; I am going over to see my father-in-law."

These short observations did not permit of discussion; a "Yes" or "No," extracted from his interlocutor, the conversation dropped dead. Then M. de Bargeton mutely implored his visitor to come to his assistance. Turning westward his old asthmatic pug-dog countenance, he gazed at you with big, lustreless eyes, in a way that said, "You were saying?"

The people whom he loved best were bores anxious to talk about themselves; he listened to them with an unfeigned and delicate interest which so endeared him to the species that all the twaddlers of Angouleme credited M. de

Bargeton with more understanding than he chose to show, and were of the opinion that he was underrated. So it happened that when these persons could find nobody else to listen to them, they went off to give M. de Bargeton the benefit of the rest of the story, argument, or what not, sure beforehand of his eulogistic smile. Madame de Bargeton's rooms were always crowded, and generally her husband felt quite at ease. He interested himself in the smallest details; he watched those who came in and bowed and smiled, and brought the new arrivals to his wife; he lay in wait for departing visitors, and went with them to the door, taking leave of them with that eternal smile. When conversation grew lively, and he saw that every one was interested in one thing or another, he stood, happy and mute, planted like a swan on both feet, listening, to all appearance, to a political discussion; or he looked over the card-players' hands without a notion of what it was all about, for he could not play at any game; or he walked about and took snuff to promote digestion. Anais was the bright side of his life; she made it unspeakably pleasant for him. Stretched out at full length in his armchair, he watched admiringly while she did her part as hostess, for she talked for him. It was a pleasure, too, to him to try to see the point in her remarks; and as it was often a good while before he succeeded, his smiles appeared after a delay, like the explosion of a shell which has entered the earth and worked up again. His respect for his wife, moreover, almost amounted to adoration. And so long as we can adore, is there not happiness enough in life? Anais' husband was as docile as a child who asks nothing better than to be told what to do; and, generous and clever woman as she was, she had taken no undue advantage of his weaknesses. She had taken care of him as you take care of a cloak; she kept him brushed, neat, and tidy, looked closely after him, and humored him; and humored, looked after, brushed, kept tidy, and cared for, M. de Bargeton had come to feel an almost dog-like affection for his wife. It is so easy to give happiness that costs nothing! Mme. de Bargeton, knowing that her husband had no pleasure but in good cheer, saw that he had good dinners; she had pity upon him, she had never uttered a word of complaint; indeed, there were people who could not understand that a woman might keep silence through pride, and argued that M. de Bargeton must possess good qualities hidden from public view. Mme. de Bargeton had drilled him into military subordination; he yielded a passive obedience to his wife. "Go and call on Monsieur So-and-So or Madame Such-an-One," she would say, and he went forthwith, like a soldier at the word of command. He stood at attention in her presence, and waited motionless for his orders.

There was some talk about this time of nominating the mute gentleman for a deputy. Lucien as yet had not lifted the veil which hid such an unimaginable character; indeed, he had scarcely frequented the house long enough. M. de Bargeton, spread at full length in his great chair, appeared to see and understand all that was going on; his silence added to his dignity, and his figure inspired Lucien with a prodigious awe. It is the wont of imaginative natures to magnify everything, or to find a soul to inhabit every shape; and Lucien took this gentleman, not for a granite guard-post, but for a formidable sphinx, and thought it necessary to conciliate him.

"I am the first comer," he said, bowing with more respect than people usually showed the worthy man.

"That is natural enough," said M. de Bargeton.

Lucien took the remark for an epigram; the lady's husband was jealous, he thought; he reddened under it, looked in the glass and tried to give himself a countenance.

"You live in L'Houmeau," said M. de Bargeton, "and people who live a long way off always come earlier than those who live near by."

"What is the reason of that?" asked Lucien politely.

"I don't know," answered M. de Bargeton, relapsing into immobility.

"You have not cared to find out," Lucien began again; "any one who could make an observation could discover the cause."

"Ah!" said M. de Bargeton, "final causes! Eh! eh!..."

The conversation came to a dead stop; Lucien racked his brains to resuscitate it.

"Mme. de Bargeton is dressing, no doubt," he began, shuddering at the silliness of the question.

"Yes, she is dressing," her husband naturally answered.

Lucien looked up at the ceiling and vainly tried to think of something else to say. As his eyes wandered over the gray painted joists and the spaces of plaster between, he saw, not without qualms, that the little chandelier with the old-fashioned cut-glass pendants had been stripped of its gauze covering and filled with wax candles. All the covers had been removed from the furniture, and the faded flowered silk damask had come to light. These preparations meant something extraordinary. The poet looked at his boots, and misgivings about his costume arose in his mind. Grown stupid with dismay, he turned and fixed his eyes on a Japanese jar standing on a begarlanded console table of the time of Louis Quinze; then, recollecting that he must conciliate Mme. de Bargeton's husband, he tried to find out if the good gentleman had a hobby of any sort in which he might be humored.

"You seldom leave the city, monsieur?" he began, returning to M. de Bargeton.

"Very seldom."

Silence again. M. de Bargeton watched Lucien's slightest movements like a suspicious cat; the young man's presence disturbed him. Each was afraid of the other.

"Can he feel suspicious of my attentions?" thought Lucien; "he seems to be anything but friendly."

Lucien was not a little embarrassed by the uneasy glances that the other gave him as he went to and fro, when luckily for him, the old man-servant (who wore livery for the occasion) announced "M. du Chatelet." The Baron came in, very much at ease, greeted his friend Bargeton, and favored Lucien with the little nod then in vogue, which the poet in his mind called purse-proud impertinence.

Sixte du Chatelet appeared in a pair of dazzling white trousers with invisible straps that kept them in shape. He wore pumps and thread stockings; the black ribbon of his eyeglass meandered over a white waistcoat, and the fashion and elegance of Paris was strikingly apparent in his black coat. He was indeed just the faded beau who might be expected from his antecedents, though advancing years had already endowed him with a certain waist-girth which somewhat exceeded the limits of elegance. He had dyed the hair and whiskers grizzled by his sufferings during his travels, and this gave a hard look to his face. The skin which had once been so delicate had been tanned to the copper-red color of Europeans from India; but in spite of his absurd pretensions to youth, you could still discern traces of the Imperial Highness' charming private secretary in du Chatelet's general appearance. He put up his eyeglass and stared at his rival's nankeen trousers, at his boots, at his waistcoat, at the blue coat made by the Angouleme tailor, he looked him over from head to foot, in short, then he coolly returned his eyeglass to his waistcoat pocket with a gesture that said, "I am satisfied." And Lucien, eclipsed at this moment by the elegance of the inland revenue department, thought that it would be his turn by and by, when he should turn a face lighted up with poetry upon the assembly; but this prospect did not prevent him from feeling the sharp pang that succeeded to the uncomfortable sense of M. de Bargeton's imagined hostility. The Baron seemed to bring all the weight of his fortune to bear upon him, the better to humiliate him in his poverty. M. de Bargeton had counted on having no more to say, and his soul was dismayed by the pause spent by the rivals in mutual survey; he had a question which he kept for desperate emergencies, laid up in his mind, as it were, against a rainy day. Now was the proper time to bring it out.

"Well, monsieur," he said, looking at Chatelet with an important air, "is there anything fresh? anything that people are talking about?"

"Why, the latest thing is M. Chardon," Chatelet said maliciously. "Ask him. Have you brought some charming poet for us?" inquired the vivacious Baron, adjusting the side curl that had gone astray on his temple.

"I should have asked you whether I had succeeded," Lucien answered; "you have been before me in the field of verse."

"Pshaw!" said the other, "a few vaudevilles, well enough in their way, written to oblige, a song now and again to suit some occasion, lines for music, no good without the music, and my long Epistle to a Sister of Bonaparte (ungrateful that he was), will not hand down my name to posterity."

At this moment Mme. de Bargeton appeared in all the glory of an elaborate toilette. She wore a Jewess' turban, enriched with an Eastern clasp. The cameos on her neck gleamed through the gauze scarf gracefully wound about her shoulders; the sleeves of her printed muslin dress were short so as to display a series of bracelets on her shapely white arms. Lucien was charmed with this theatrical style of dress. M. du Chatelet gallantly plied the queen with fulsome compliments, that made her smile with pleasure; she was so glad to be praised in Lucien's hearing. But she scarcely gave her dear poet a glance, and met Chatelet with a mortifying civility that kept him at a distance.

By this time the guests began to arrive. First and foremost appeared the Bishop and his Vicar-General, dignified and reverend figures both, though no two men could well be more unlike, his lordship being tall and attenuated, and his acolyte short and fat. Both churchmen's eyes were bright; but while the Bishop was pallid, his Vicar-General's countenance glowed with high health. Both were impassive, and gesticulated but little; both appeared to be prudent men, and their silence and reserve were supposed to hide great intellectual powers.

Close upon the two ecclesiastics followed Mme. de Chandour and her husband, a couple so extraordinary that those who are unfamiliar with provincial life might be tempted to think that such persons are purely imaginary. Amelie de Chandour posed as the rival queen of Angouleme; her husband, M. de Chandour, known in the circle as Stanislas, was a *ci-devant* young man, slim still at five-and-forty, with a countenance like a sieve. His cravat was always tied so as to present two menacing points – one spike reached the height of his right ear, the other pointed downwards to the red ribbon of his cross. His coat-tails were violently at strife. A cut-away waistcoat displayed the ample, swelling curves of a stiffly-starched shirt fastened by massive gold studs. His dress, in fact, was exaggerated, till he looked almost like a living caricature, which no one could behold for the first time with gravity.

Stanislas looked himself over from top to toe with a kind of satisfaction; he verified the number of his waistcoat buttons, and followed the curving outlines of his tight-fitting trousers with fond glances that came to a standstill at last on the pointed tips of his shoes. When he ceased to contemplate himself in this way, he looked towards the nearest mirror to see if his hair still kept in curl; then, sticking a finger in his waistcoat pocket, he looked about him at the women with happy eyes, flinging his head back in three-quarters profile with all the airs of a king of the poultry-yard, airs which were prodigiously admired by the aristocratic circle of which he was the beau. There was a strain of eighteenth century grossness, as a rule, in his talk; a detestable kind of conversation which procured him some success with women – he made them laugh. M. du Chatelet was beginning to give this gentleman some uneasiness; and, as a matter of fact, since Mme. de Bargeton had taken him up, the lively interest taken by the women in the Byron of Angouleme was distinctly on the increase. His coxcomb superciliousness tickled their curiosity; he posed as the man whom nothing can arouse from his apathy, and his jaded Sultan airs were like a challenge.

Amelie de Chandour, short, plump, fair-complexioned, and dark-haired, was a poor actress; her voice was loud, like everything else about her; her head, with its load of feathers in winter and flowers in summer, was never still for a moment. She had a fine flow of conversation, though she could never bring a sentence to an end without a wheezing accompaniment from an asthma, to which she would not confess.

M. de Saintot, otherwise Astolphe, President of the Agricultural Society, a tall, stout, high-colored personage, usually appeared in the wake of his wife, Elisa, a lady with a countenance like a withered fern, called Lili by her friends – a baby name singularly at variance with its owner's character and demeanor. Mme. de Saintot was a solemn and extremely pious woman, and a very trying partner at a game of cards. Astolphe was supposed to be a scientific man of the first rank. He was as ignorant as a carp, but he had compiled the articles on Sugar and Brandy for a Dictionary of Agriculture by wholesale plunder of newspaper articles and pillage of previous writers. It was believed all over the department that M. Saintot was engaged upon a treatise on modern husbandry; but though he locked himself into his study every morning, he had not written a couple of pages in a dozen years. If anybody called to see him, he always contrived to be discovered rummaging among his papers, hunting for a stray note or mending a pen; but he spent the whole time in his study on puerilities, reading the newspaper through from end to end, cutting figures out of corks with his penknife, and drawing patterns on his blotting-paper. He would turn over the leaves of his Cicero to see if any-thing applicable to the events of the day might catch his eye, and drag his quotation by the heels into the conversation that evening saying, "There is a passage in Cicero which might have been written to suit modern times," and out came his phrase, to the astonishment of his au-dience. "Really," they said among themselves, "Astolphe is a well of learning." The interesting fact circulated all over the town, and sustained the general belief in M. de Saintot's abilities.

After this pair came M. de Bartas, known as Adrien among the circle. It was M. de Bartas who boomed out his song in a bass voice, and made prodigious claims to musical knowledge. His self-conceit had taken a stand upon solfeggi; he began by admiring his appearance while he sang, passed thence to talking about music, and finally to talking of nothing else. His musical tastes had become a monomania; he grew ani-mated only on the one subject of music; he was miserable all evening until somebody begged him to sing. When he had bellowed one of his airs, he revived again; strutted about, raised himself on his heels, and received compliments with a deprecating air; but modesty did not prevent him from going from group to group for his meed of praise; and when there was no more to be said about the singer, he returned to the subject of the song, discussing its difficulties or extolling the composer.

M. Alexandre de Brebian performed heroic exploits in sepia; he disfigured the walls of his friends' rooms with a swarm of crude productions, and spoiled all the albums in the department. M. Alexandre de Brebian and M. de Bartas came together, each with his friend's wife on his arm, a cross-cornered arrangement which gossip declared to be carried out to the fullest extent. As for the two women, Mesdames Charlotte de Brebian and Josephine de Bartas, or Lolotte and Fifine, as they were called, both took an equal interest in a scarf, or the trimming of a dress, or the reconciliation of several irreconcilable colors; both were eaten up with a desire to look like Parisiennes, and neglected their homes, where everything went wrong. But if they dressed like dolls in tightly-fitting gowns of home manufacture, and exhibited outrageous combinations of crude colors upon their persons, their husbands availed themselves of the artist's privilege and dressed as they pleased, and curious it was to see the provincial dowdiness of the pair. In their threadbare clothes they looked like the supernumeraries that represent rank and fashion at stage weddings in third-rate theatres.

One of the queerest figures in the rooms was M. le Comte de Senonches, known by the aristocratic name of Jacques, a mighty hunter, lean and sunburned, a haughty gentleman, about as amiable as a wild boar, as suspicious as a Venetian, and jealous as a Moor, who lived on terms of the friendliest and most perfect intimacy with M. du Hautoy, otherwise Francis, the friend of the house.

Madame de Senonches (Zephirine) was a tall, fine-looking woman, though her complexion was spoiled already by pimples due to liver complaint, on which grounds she was said to be exacting. With a slender figure and delicate proportions, she could afford to indulge in languid manners, savoring somewhat of affectation, but revealing passion and the consciousness that every least caprice will be gratified by love.

Francis, the house friend, was rather distinguished-looking. He had given up his consulship in Valence, and sacrificed his diplomatic prospects to live near Zephirine[1] in Angouleme. He had taken the household in charge, he superintended the children's education, taught them foreign languages, and looked after the fortunes

---

[1] also known as Zizine

of M. and Mme. de Senonches with the most complete devotion. Noble Angouleme, administrative Angouleme, and *bourgeois* Angouleme alike had looked askance for a long while at this phenomenon of the perfect union of three persons; but finally the mysterious conjugal trinity appeared to them so rare and pleasing a spectacle, that if M. du Hautoy had shown any intention of marrying, he would have been thought monstrously immoral. Mme. de Senonches, however, had a lady companion, a goddaughter, and her excessive attachment to this Mlle. de la Haye was beginning to raise surmises of disquieting mysteries; it was thought, in spite of some impossible discrepancies in dates, that Francoise de la Haye bore a striking likeness to Francis du Hautoy.

When "Jacques" was shooting in the neighborhood, people used to inquire after Francis, and Jacques would discourse on his steward's little ailments, and talk of his wife in the second place. So curious did this blindness seem in a man of jealous temper, that his greatest friends used to draw him out on the topic for the amusement of others who did not know of the mystery. M. du Hautoy was a finical dandy whose minute care of himself had degenerated into mincing affectation and childishness. He took an interest in his cough, his appetite, his digestion, his night's rest. Zephirine had succeeded in making a valetudinarian of her factotum; she coddled him and doctored him; she crammed him with delicate fare, as if he had been a fine lady's lap-dog; she embroidered waistcoats for him, and pocket-handkerchiefs and cravats until he became so used to wearing finery that she transformed him into a kind of Japanese idol. Their understanding was perfect. In season and out of season Zizine consulted Francis with a look, and Francis seemed to take his ideas from Zizine's eyes. They frowned and smiled together, and seemingly took counsel of each other before making the simplest commonplace remark.

The largest landowner in the neighborhood, a man whom every one envied, was the Marquis de Pimentel; he and his wife, between them, had an income of forty thousand livres, and spent their winters in Paris. This evening they had driven into Angouleme in their caleche, and had brought their neighbors, the Baron and Baroness de Rastignac and their party, the Baroness' aunt and daughters, two charming young ladies, penniless girls who had been carefully brought up, and were dressed in the simple way that sets off natural loveliness.

These personages, beyond question the first in the company, met with a reception of chilling silence; the respect paid to them was full of jealousy, especially as everybody saw that Mme. de Bargeton paid marked attention to the guests. The two families belonged to the very small minority who hold themselves aloof from provincial gossip, belong to no clique, live quietly in retirement, and maintain a dignified reserve. M. de Pimentel and M. de Rastignac, for instance, were addressed by their names in full, and no length of acquaintance had brought their wives and daughters into the select coterie of Angouleme; both families were too nearly connected with the Court to compromise themselves through provincial follies.

The Prefect and the General in command of the garrison were the last comers, and with them came the country gentleman who had brought the treatise on silkworms to David that very morning. Evidently he was the mayor of some canton or other, and a fine estate was his sufficient title to gentility; but from his appearance, it was plain that he was quite unused to polite society. He looked uneasy in his clothes, he was at a loss to know what to do with his hands, he shifted about from one foot to another as he spoke, and half rose and sat down again when anybody spoke to him. He seemed ready to do some menial service; he was obsequious, nervous, and grave by turns, laughing eagerly at every joke, listening with servility; and occasionally, imagining that people were laughing at him, he assumed a knowing air. His treatise weighed upon his mind; again and again he tried to talk about silkworms; but the luckless wight happened first upon M. de Bartas, who talked music in reply, and next on M. de Saintot, who quoted Cicero to him; and not until the evening was half over did the mayor meet with sympathetic listeners in Mme. and Mlle. du Brossard, a widowed gentlewoman and her daughter.

Mme. and Mlle. du Brossard were not the least interesting persons in the clique, but their story may be told in a single phrase – they were as poor as they were noble. In their dress there was just that tinge of pretension which betrayed carefully hidden penury. The daughter, a big, heavy young woman of seven-and-twenty, was supposed to be a good performer on the piano, and her mother praised her in season and out of season in the clumsiest way. No eligible man had any taste which Camille did not share on her mother's authoritative statement. Mme. du Brossard, in her anxiety to establish her child, was capable of saying that her dear Camille liked nothing so much as a roving life from one garrison to another; and before the evening was out, that she was sure her dear Camille liked a quiet country farmhouse existence of all things. Mother and daughter had the pinched sub-acid dignity characteristic of those who have learned by experience the exact value of expressions of sympathy; they belonged to a class which the world delights to pity; they had been the objects of the benevolent interest of egoism; they had sounded the empty void beneath the consoling formulas with which the world ministers to the necessities of the unfortunate.

M. de Severac was fifty-nine years old, and a childless widower. Mother and daughter listened, therefore, with devout admiration to all that he told them about his silkworm nurseries.

"My daughter has always been fond of animals," said the mother. "And as women are especially interested in the silk which the little creatures produce, I shall ask permission to go over to Severac, so that my Camille may see how the silk is spun. My Camille is so intelligent, she will grasp anything that you tell her in a moment. Did she not understand one day the inverse ratio of the squares of distances!"

This was the remark that brought the conversation between Mme. du Brossard and M. de Severac to a glorious close after Lucien's reading that night.

A few habitues slipped in familiarly among the rest, so did one or two eldest sons; shy, mute young men tricked out in gorgeous jewelry, and highly honored by an invitation to this literary solemnity, the boldest men among them so far shook off the weight of awe as to chatter a good deal with Mlle. de la Haye. The women solemnly arranged themselves in a circle, and the men stood behind them. It was a quaint assemblage of wrinkled countenances and heterogeneous costumes, but none the less it seemed very alarming to Lucien, and his heart beat fast when he felt that every one was looking at him. His assurance bore the ordeal with some difficulty in spite of the encouraging example of Mme. de Bargeton, who welcomed the most illustrious personages of Angouleme with ostentatious courtesy and elaborate graciousness; and the uncomfortable feeling that oppressed him was aggravated by a trifling matter which any one might have foreseen, though it was bound to come as an unpleasant shock to a young man with so little experience of the world. Lucien, all eyes and ears, noticed that no one except Louise, M. de Bargeton, the Bishop, and some few who wished to please the mistress of the house, spoke of him as M. de Rubempre; for his formidable audience he was M. Chardon. Lucien's courage sank under their inquisitive eyes. He could read his plebeian name in the mere movements of their lips, and hear the anticipatory criticisms made in the blunt, provincial fashion that too often borders on rudeness. He had not expected this prolonged ordeal of pin-pricks; it put him still more out of humor with himself. He grew impatient to begin the reading, for then he could assume an attitude which should put an end to his mental torments; but Jacques was giving Mme. de Pimentel the history of his last day's sport; Adrien was holding forth to Mlle. Laure de Rastignac on Rossini, the newly-risen music star, and Astolphe, who had got by heart a newspaper paragraph on a patent plow, was giving the Baron the benefit of the description. Lucien, luckless poet that he was, did not know that there was scarce a soul in the room besides

Mme. de Bargeton who could understand poetry. The whole matter-of-fact assembly was there by a misapprehension, nor did they, for the most part, know what they had come out for to see. There are some words that draw a public as unfailingly as the clash of cymbals, the trumpet, or the mountebank's big drum; "beauty," "glory," "poetry," are words that bewitch the coarsest intellect.

When every one had arrived; when the buzz of talk ceased after repeated efforts on the part of M. de Bargeton, who, obedient to his wife, went round the room much as the beadle makes the circle of the church, tapping the pavement with his wand; when silence, in fact, was at last secured, Lucien went to the round table near Mme. de Bargeton. A fierce thrill of excitement ran through him as he did so. He announced in an uncertain voice that, to prevent disappointment, he was about to read the masterpieces of a great poet, discovered only recently (for although Andre de Chenier's poems appeared in 1819, no one in Angouleme had so much as heard of him). Everybody interpreted this announcement in one way – it was a shift of Mme. de Bargeton's, meant to save the poet's self-love and to put the audience at ease.

Lucien began with *Le Malade*, and the poem was received with a murmur of applause; but he followed it with *L'Aveugle*, which proved too great a strain upon the average intellect. None but

artists or those endowed with the artistic temperament can understand and sympathize with him
in the diabolical torture of that reading. If poetry
is to be rendered by the voice, and if the listener
is to grasp all that it means, the most devout
attention is essential; there should be an intimate alliance between the reader and his audience, or swift and subtle communication of the
poet's thought and feeling becomes impossible.
Here this close sympathy was lacking, and Lucien
in consequence was in the position of an angel
who should endeavor to sing of heaven amid the
chucklings of hell. An intelligent man in the
sphere most stimulating to his faculties can see
in every direction, like a snail; he has the keen
scent of a dog, the ears of a mole; he can hear,
and feel, and see all that is going on around
him. A musician or a poet knows at once whether
his audience is listening in admiration or fails to
follow him, and feels it as the plant that revives
or droops under favorable or unfavorable conditions. The men who had come with their wives
had fallen to discussing their own affairs; by the
acoustic law before mentioned, every murmur
rang in Lucien's ear; he saw all the gaps caused
by the spasmodic workings of jaws sympatheti-
cally affected, the teeth that seemed to grin de-
fiance at him.

When, like the dove in the deluge, he looked
round for any spot on which his eyes might rest,
he saw nothing but rows of impatient faces. Their
owners clearly were waiting for him to make an

end; they had come together to discuss questions of practical interest. With the exceptions of Laure de Rastignac, the Bishop, and two or three of the young men, they one and all looked bored. As a matter of fact, those who understand poetry strive to develop the germs of another poetry, quickened within them by the poet's poetry; but this glacial audience, so far from attaining to the spirit of the poet, did not even listen to the letter.

Lucien felt profoundly discouraged; he was damp with chilly perspiration; a glowing glance from Louise, to whom he turned, gave him courage to persevere to the end, but this poet's heart was bleeding from countless wounds.

"Do you find this very amusing, Fifine?" inquired the wizened Lili, who perhaps had expected some kind of gymnastics.

"Don't ask me what I think, dear; I cannot keep my eyes open when any one begins to read aloud."

"I hope that Nais will not give us poetry often in the evenings," said Francis. "If I am obliged to attend while somebody reads aloud after dinner, it upsets my digestion."

"Poor dearie," whispered Zephirine, "take a glass of eau *sucree*."

"It was very well declaimed," said Alexandre, "but I like whist better myself."

After this dictum, which passed muster as a joke from the play on the word "whist," several card-players were of the opinion that the reader's voice needed a rest, and on this pretext one or two couples slipped away into the card-room. But Louise, and the Bishop, and pretty Laure de Rastignac besought Lucien to continue, and this time he caught the attention of his audience with Chenier's spirited reactionary *Iambes*. Several persons, carried away by his impassioned delivery, applauded the reading without understanding the sense. People of this sort are impressed by vociferation, as a coarse palate is ticked by strong spirits.

During the interval, as they partook of ices, Zephirine despatched Francis to examine the volume, and informed her neighbor Amelie that the poetry was in print.

Amelie brightened visibly.

"Why, that is easily explained," said she. "M. de Rubempre works for a printer. It is as if a pretty woman should make her own dresses," she added, looking at Lolotte.

"He printed his poetry himself!" said the women among themselves.

"Then, why does he call himself M. de Rubempre?" inquired Jacques. "If a noble takes a handicraft, he ought to lay his name aside."

"So he did as a matter of fact," said Zizine, "but his name was plebeian, and he took his mother's name, which is noble."

"Well, if his verses are printed, we can read them for ourselves," said Astolphe.

This piece of stupidity complicated the question, until Sixte du Chatelet condescended to inform these unlettered folk that the prefatory announcement was no oratorical flourish, but a statement of fact, and added that the poems had been written by a Royalist brother of Marie-Joseph Chenier, the Revolutionary leader. All Angouleme, except Mme. de Rastignac and her two daughters and the Bishop, who had really felt the grandeur of the poetry, were mystified, and took offence at the hoax. There was a smothered murmur, but Lucien did not heed it. The intoxication of the poetry was upon him; he was far away from the hateful world, striving to render in speech the music that filled his soul, seeing the faces about him through a cloudy haze. He read the sombre Elegy on the Suicide, lines in the taste of a by-gone day, pervaded by sublime melancholy; then he turned to the page where the line occurs, "Thy songs are sweet, I love to say them over," and ended with the delicate idyll Neere.

Mme. de Bargeton sat with one hand buried in her curls, heedless of the havoc she wrought among them, gazing before her with unseeing eyes, alone in her drawing-room, lost in delicious dreaming; for the first time in her life she had been transported to the sphere which was hers by right of nature. Judge, therefore, how unpleasantly she was disturbed by Amelie, who took it upon herself to express the general wish.

"Nais," this voice broke in, "we came to hear M. Chardon's poetry, and you are giving us poetry out of a book. The extracts are very nice, but the ladies feel a patriotic preference for the wine of the country; they would rather have it."

"The French language does not lend itself very readily to poetry, does it?" Astolphe remarked to Chatelet. "Cicero's prose is a thousand times more poetical to my way of thinking."

"The true poetry of France is song, lyric verse," Chatelet answered.

"Which proves that our language is eminently adapted for music," said Adrien.

"I should like very much to hear the poetry that has cost Nais her reputation," said Zephirine; "but after receiving Amelie's request in such a way, it is not very likely that she will give us a specimen."

"She ought to have them recited in justice to herself," said Francis. "The little fellow's genius is his sole justification."

"You have been in the diplomatic service," said Amelie to M. du Chatelet, "go and manage it somehow."

"Nothing easier," said the Baron.

The Princess' private secretary, being accustomed to petty manoeuvres of this kind, went to the Bishop and contrived to bring him to the fore. At the Bishop's entreaty, Nais had no choice but to ask Lucien to recite his own verses for them, and the Baron received a languishing smile from Amelie as the reward of his prompt success.

"Decidedly, the Baron is a very clever man," she observed to Lolotte.

But Amelie's previous acidulous remark about women who made their own dresses rankled in Lolotte's mind.

"Since when have you begun to recognize the Emperor's barons?" she asked, smiling.

Lucien had essayed to deify his beloved in an ode, dedicated to her under a title in favor with all lads who write verse after leaving school. This ode, so fondly cherished, so beautiful – since it was the outpouring of all the love in his heart, seemed to him to be the one piece of his own work that could hold its own with Chenier's verse; and with a tolerably fatuous glance at Mme. de Bargeton, he announced "TO HER!" He struck an attitude proudly for the delivery of the ambitious piece, for his author's self-love felt safe and at ease behind Mme. de Bargeton's petticoat. And at the selfsame moment Mme. de Bargeton betrayed her own secret to the women's curious eyes. Although she had always looked down upon this audience from her own loftier intellectual heights, she could not help trembling for Lucien. Her face was troubled, there was a sort of mute appeal for indulgence in her glances, and while the verses were recited she was obliged to lower her eyes and dissemble her pleasure as stanza followed stanza.

TO HER.

Out of the glowing heart of the torrent of glory and light,

At the foot of Jehovah's throne where the angels stand afar,

Each on a seistron of gold repeating the prayers of the night,

Put up for each by his star.

Out from the cherubim choir a bright-haired Angel springs,

Veiling the glory of God that dwells on a dazzling brow,

Leaving the courts of heaven to sink upon silver wings

Down to our world below.

God looked in pity on earth, and the Angel, reading His thought,

Came down to lull the pain of the mighty spirit at strife,

Reverent bent o'er the maid, and for age left desolate brought

Flowers of the springtime of life.

Bringing a dream of hope to solace the mother's fears,

Hearkening unto the voice of the tardy re- pentant cry,

Glad as angels are glad, to reckon Earth's pitying tears,

Given with alms of a sigh.

One there is, and but one, bright messenger sent from the skies

Whom earth like a lover fain would hold
from the hea'nward flight;

But the angel, weeping, turns and gazes
with sad, sweet eyes

Up to the heaven of light.

Not by the radiant eyes, not by the kindling
glow

Of virtue sent from God, did I know the
secret sign,

Nor read the token sent on a white and
dazzling brow

Of an origin divine.

Nay, it was Love grown blind and dazed
with excess of light,

Striving and striving in vain to mingle Earth
and Heaven,

Helpless and powerless against the invinci-
ble armor bright

By the dread archangel given.

Ah! be wary, take heed, lest aught should
be seen or heard

Of the shining seraph band, as they
take the heavenward way;

Too soon the Angel on Earth will learn
the magical word

Sung at the close of the day.

Then you shall see afar, rifting the
darkness of night,

A gleam as of dawn that spread across
the starry floor,

And the seaman that watch for a sign
shall mark the track of their flight,

A luminous pathway in Heaven and a
beacon for evermore.

"Do you read the riddle?" said Amelie, giving
M. du Chatelet a coquettish glance.

"It is the sort of stuff that we all of us wrote
more or less after we left school," said the
Baron with a bored expression – he was
acting his part of arbiter of taste who has
seen everything. "We used to deal in Ossian-
ic mists, Malvinas and Fingals and cloudy
shapes, and warriors who got out of their
tombs with stars above their heads. Nowa-
days this poetical frippery has been replaced
by Jehovah, angels, seistrons, the plumes

of seraphim, and all the paraphernalia of paradise freshened up with a few new words such as 'immense, infinite, solitude, intelligence'; you have lakes, and the words of the Almighty, a kind of Christianized Pantheism, enriched with the most extraordinary and unheard-of rhymes. We are in quite another latitude, in fact; we have left the North for the East, but the darkness is just as thick as before."

"If the ode is obscure, the declaration is very clear, it seems to me," said Zephirine.

"And the archangel's armor is a tolerably thin gauze robe," said Francis.

Politeness demanded that the audience should profess to be enchanted with the poem; and the women, furious because they had no poets in their train to extol them as angels, rose, looked bored by the reading, murmuring, "Very nice!" "Charming!" "Perfect!" with frigid coldness.

"If you love me, do not congratulate the poet or his angel," Lolotte laid her commands on her dear Adrien in imperious tones, and Adrien was fain to obey.

"Empty words, after all," Zephirine remarked to Francis, "and love is a poem that we live."

"You have just expressed the very thing that I was thinking, Zizine, but I should not have put it so neatly," said Stanislas, scanning himself from top to toe with loving attention.

"I would give, I don't know how much, to see Nais' pride brought down a bit," said Amelie, addressing Chatelet. "Nais sets up to be an archangel, as if she were better than the rest of us, and mixes us up with low people; his father was an apothecary, and his mother is a nurse; his sister works in a laundry, and he himself is a printer's foreman."

"If his father sold biscuits for worms" (*vers*), said Jacques, "he ought to have made his son take them."

"He is continuing in his father's line of business, for the stuff that he has just been reading to us is a drug in the market, it seems," said Stanislas, striking one of his most killing attitudes. "Drug for drug, I would rather have something else."

Every one apparently combined to humiliate Lucien by various aristocrats' sarcasms. Lili the religious thought it a charitable deed to use any means of enlightening Nais, and Nais was on the brink of a piece of folly. Francis the diplomatist undertook the direction of the silly conspiracy; every one was interested in the progress of the drama; it would be something to talk about to-morrow. The ex-consul, being far from anxious to engage in a duel with a young poet who would fly into a rage at the first hint of insult under his lady's eyes, was wise enough to see that the only way of dealing Lucien his deathblow was by the spiritual arm which was safe from vengeance. He therefore followed the example set by Chatelet the astute, and went to the Bishop. Him he proceeded to mystify.

He told the Bishop that Lucien's mother was a woman of uncommon powers and great modesty, and that it was she who found the subjects for her son's verses. Nothing pleased Lucien so much, according to the guileful Francis, as any recognition of her talents – he worshiped his mother. Then, having inculcated these notions, he left the rest to time. His lordship was sure to bring out the insulting allusion, for which he had been so carefully prepared, in the course of conversation.

When Francis and the Bishop joined the little group where Lucien stood, the circle who gave him the cup of hemlock to drain by little sips watched him with redoubled interest. The poet, luckless young man, being a total stranger, and unaware of the manners and customs of the house, could only look at Mme. de Bargeton and give embarrassed answers to embarrassing questions. He knew neither the names nor condition of the people about him; the women's silly speeches made him blush for them, and he was at his wits' end for a reply. He felt, moreover, how very far removed he was from these divinities of Angouleme when he heard himself addressed sometimes as M. Chardon, sometimes as M. de Rubempre, while they addressed each other as Lolotte, Adrien, Astolphe, Lili and Fifine. His confusion rose to a height when, taking Lili for a man's surname, he addressed the coarse M. de Senonches as M. Lili; that Nimrod broke in upon him with a " *MONSIEUR LULU?"* and Mme. de Bargeton flushed red to the eyes.

"A woman must be blind indeed to bring this little fellow among us!" muttered Senonches.

Zephirine turned to speak to the Marquise de Pimentel – "Do you not see a strong likeness between M. Chardon and M. de Cante-Croix, madame?" she asked in a low but quite audible voice.

"The likeness is ideal," smiled Mme. de Pimentel.

"Glory has a power of attraction to which we can confess," said Mme. de Bargeton, address-ing the Marquise. "Some women are as much attracted by greatness as others by littleness," she added, looking at Francis.

The was beyond Zephirine's comprehension; she thought her consul a very great man; but the Marquise laughed, and her laughter ranged her on Nais' side.

"You are very fortunate, monsieur," said the Marquis de Pimentel, addressing Lucien for the purpose of calling him M. de Rubempre, and not M. Chardon, as before; "you should never find time heavy on your hands."

"Do you work quickly?" asked Lolotte, much in the way that she would have asked a joiner "if it took long to make a box."

The bludgeon stroke stunned Lucien, but he raised his head at Mme. de Bargeton's reply-

"My dear, poetry does not grow in M. de Rubempre's head like grass in our courtyards."

"Madame, we cannot feel too reverently towards the noble spirits in whom God has set some ray of this light," said the Bishop, addressing Lolotte. "Yes, poetry is something holy. Poetry implies suffering. How many silent nights those verses that you admire have cost! We should bow in love and reverence before the poet; his life here is almost always a life of sorrow; but God doubtless reserves a place in heaven for him among His prophets. This young man is a poet," he added laying a hand on Lucien's head; "do you not see the sign of Fate set on that high forehead of his?"

Glad to be so generously championed, Lucien made his acknowledgments in a grateful look, not knowing that the worthy prelate was to deal his deathblow.

Mme. de Bargeton's eyes traveled round the hostile circle. Her glances went like arrows to the depths of her rivals' hearts, and left them twice as furious as before.

"Ah, monseigneur," cried Lucien, hoping to break thick heads with his golden sceptre, "but ordinary people have neither your intellect nor your charity. No one heeds our sorrows, our toil is unrecognized. The gold-digger working in the mine does not labor as we to wrest metaphors from the heart of the most ungrateful of all languages. If this is poetry – to give ideas such definite and clear expressions that all the world can see and understand – the poet must continually range through the entire scale of human intellects, so that he can satisfy the demands of all; he must conceal hard thinking and emotion, two antagonistic powers, beneath the most vivid color; he must know how to make one word cover a whole world of thought; he must give the results of whole systems of philosophy in a few picturesque lines; indeed, his songs are like seeds that must break into blossom in other hearts wherever they find the soil prepared by personal experience. How can you express unless you first have felt? And is not passion suffering. Poetry is only brought forth after painful wanderings in the vast regions of thought and life. There are men and women in books, who seem more really alive to us than men and women who have lived and died – Richardson's Clarissa, Chenier's Camille, the Delia of Tibullus, Ariosto's Angelica, Dante's Francesca, Moliere's Alceste, Beaumarchais' Figaro, Scott's Rebecca the Jewess, the Don Quixote of Cervantes, – do we not owe these deathless creations to immortal throes?"

"And what are you going to create for us?" asked Chatelet.

"If I were to announce such conceptions, I should give myself out for a man of genius, should I not?" answered Lucien. "And besides, such sublime creations demand a long experience of the world and a study of human passion and interests which I could not possibly have made; but I have made a beginning," he added, with bitterness in his tone, as he took a vengeful glance round the circle; "the time of gestation is long..."

"Then it will be a case of difficult labor," interrupted M. du Hautoy.

"Your excellent mother might assist you," suggested the Bishop.

The epigram, innocently made by the good prelate, the long-looked-for revenge, kindled a gleam of delight in all eyes. The smile of satisfied caste that traveled from mouth to mouth was aggravated by M. de Bargeton's imbecility; he burst into a laugh, as usual, some moments later.

"Monseigneur, you are talking a little above our heads; these ladies do not understand your meaning," said Mme. de Bargeton, and the words paralyzed the laughter, and drew astonished eyes upon her. "A poet who looks to the Bible for his inspiration has a mother indeed in the Church. – M. de Rubempre, will you recite *Saint John in Patmos* for us, or *Belshazzar's Feast*, so that his lordship may see that Rome is still the *Magna Parens* of Virgil?"

The women exchanged smiles at the Latin words.

The bravest and highest spirits know times of prostration at the outset of life. Lucien had sunk to the depths at the blow, but he struck the bottom with his feet, and rose to the surface again, vowing to subjugate this little world. He rose like a bull, stung to fury by a shower of darts, and prepared to obey Louise by declaiming *Saint John in Patmos*; but by this time the card-tables had claimed their complement of players, who returned to the accustomed groove to find amusement there which poetry had not afforded them. They felt besides that the revenge of so many outraged vanities would be incomplete unless it were followed up by contemptuous indifference; so they showed their tacit disdain for the native product by leaving Lucien and Mme. de Bargeton to themselves. Every one appeared to be absorbed in his own affairs; one chattered with the prefect about a new crossroad, another proposed to vary the pleasures of the evening with a little music. The great world of Angouleme, feeling that it was no judge of poetry, was very anxious, in the first place, to hear the verdict of the Pimentels and the Rastignacs, and formed a little group about them. The great influence wielded in the department by these two families was always felt on every important occasion; every one was jealous of them, every one paid court to them, foreseeing that they might some day need that influence.

"What do you think of our poet and his poetry?" Jacques asked of the Marquise. Jacques used to shoot over the lands belonging to the Pimentel family.

"Why, it is not bad for provincial poetry," she said, smiling; "and besides, such a beautiful poet cannot do anything amiss."

Every one thought the decision admirable; it traveled from lip to lip, gaining malignance by the way. Then Chatelet was called upon to accompany M. du Bartas on the piano while he mangled the great solo from *Figaro*; and the way being opened to music, the audience, as in duty bound listened while Chatelet in turn sang one of Chateaubriand's ballads, a chivalrous ditty made in the time of the Empire. Duets followed, of the kind usually left to boarding-school misses, and rescued from the schoolroom by Mme. du Brossard, who meant to make a brilliant display of her dear Camille's talents for M. de Severac's benefit.

Mme. du Bargeton, hurt by the contempt which every one showed her poet, paid back scorn for scorn by going to her boudoir during these performances. She was followed by the prelate. His Vicar-General had just been explaining the profound irony of the epigram into which he had been entrapped, and the Bishop wished to make amends. Mlle. de Rastignac, fascinated by the poetry, also slipped into the boudoir without her mother's knowledge.

Louise drew Lucien to her mattress-cushioned sofa; and with no one to see or hear, she murmured in his ear, "Dear angel, they did not understand you; but, 'Thy songs are sweet, I love to say them over.'"

And Lucien took comfort from the pretty speech, and forgot his woes for a little.

"Glory is not to be had cheaply," Mme. de Bargeton continued, taking his hand and holding it tightly in her own. "Endure your woes, my friend, you will be great one day; your pain is the price of your immortality. If only I had a hard struggle before me! God preserve you from the enervating life without battles, in which the eagle's wings have no room to spread themselves. I envy you; for if you suffer, at least you live. You will put out your strength, you will feel the hope of victory; your strife will be glorious. And when you shall come to your kingdom, and reach the imperial sphere where great minds are enthroned, then remember the poor creatures disinherited by fate, whose intellects pine in an oppressive moral atmosphere, who die and have never lived, knowing all the while what life might be; think of the piercing eyes that have seen nothing, the delicate senses that have only known the scent of poison flowers. Then tell in your song of plants that wither in the depths of the forest, choked by twining growths and rank, greedy vegetation, plants that have never been kissed by the sunlight, and die, never having put forth a blossom. It would be a terribly gloomy poem, would it not, a fanciful subject? What a sublime poem might be made of the story of some daughter of the desert transported to some cold, western clime, calling for her beloved sun, dying of a grief that none can understand, overcome with cold and longing. It would be an allegory; many lives are like that."

"You would picture the spirit which remembers Heaven," said the Bishop; "some one surely must have written such a poem in the days of old; I like to think that I see a fragment of it in the Song of Songs."

"Take that as your subject," said Laure de Rastignac, expressing her artless belief in Lucien's powers.

"The great sacred poem of France is still unwritten," remarked the Bishop. "Believe me, glory and success await the man of talent who shall work for religion."

"That task will be his," said Mme. de Bargeton rhetorically. "Do you not see the first beginnings of the vision of the poem, like the flame of dawn, in his eyes?"

"Nais is treating us very badly," said Fifine; "what can she be doing?"

"Don't you hear?" said Stanislas. "She is flourishing away, using big words that you cannot make head or tail of."

Amelie, Fifine, Adrien, and Francis appeared in the doorway with Mme. de Rastignac, who came to look for her daughter.

"Nais," cried the two ladies, both delighted to break in upon the quiet chat in the boudoir, "it would be very nice of you to come and play something for us."

"My dear child, M. de Rubempre is just about to recite his *Saint John in Patmos*, a magnificent biblical poem."

"Biblical!" echoed Fifine in amazement.

Amelie and Fifine went back to the drawing-room, taking the word back with them as food for laughter. Lucien pleaded a defective memory and excused himself. When he reappeared, nobody took the slightest notice of him; every one was chatting or busy at the card-tables; the poet's aureole had been plucked away, the landowners had no use for him, the more pretentious sort looked upon him as an enemy to their ignorance, while the women were jealous of Mme. de Bargeton, the Beatrice of this modern Dante, to use the Vicar-General's phrase, and looked at him with cold, scornful eyes.

"So this is society!" Lucien said to himself as he went down to L'Houmeau by the steps of Beaulieu; for there are times when we choose to take the longest way, that the physical exercise of walking may promote the flow of ideas.

So far from being disheartened, the fury of repulsed ambition gave Lucien new strength. Like all those whose instincts bring them to a higher social sphere which they reach before they can hold their own in it, Lucien vowed to make any sacrifice to the end that he might remain on that higher social level. One by one he drew out the poisoned shafts on his way home, talking aloud to himself, scoffing at the fools with whom he had to do, inventing neat answers to their idiotic questions, desperately vexed that the witty responses occurred to him so late in the day. By the time that he reached the Bordeaux road, between the river and the foot of the hill, he thought that he could see Eve and David sitting on a baulk of timber by the river in the moonlight, and went down the footpath towards them.

While Lucien was hastening to the torture in Mme. de Bargeton's rooms, his sister had changed her dress for a gown of pink cambric covered with narrow stripes, a straw hat, and a little silk shawl. The simple costume seemed like a rich toilette on Eve, for she was one of those women whose great nature lends stateliness to the least personal detail; and David felt prodigiously shy of her now that she had changed her working dress. He had made up his mind that he would speak of himself; but now as he gave his arm to this beautiful girl, and they walked through L'Houmeau together, he could find nothing to say to her. Love delights in such reverent awe as redeemed souls know on beholding the glory of God. So, in silence, the two lovers went across the Bridge of Saint Anne, and followed the left bank of the Charente. Eve felt embarrassed by the pause, and stopped to look along the river; a joyous shaft of sunset had turned the water between the bridge and the new powder mills into a sheet of gold.

"What a beautiful evening it is!" she said, for the sake of saying something; "the air is warm and fresh, and full of the scent of flowers, and there is a wonderful sky."

"Everything speaks to our heart," said David, trying to proceed to love by way of analogy. "Those who love find infinite delight in discovering the poetry of their own inmost souls in every chance effect of the landscape, in the thin, clear air, in the scent of the earth. Nature speaks for them."

"And loosens their tongues, too," Eve said merrily. "You were very silent as we came through L'Houmeau. Do you know, I felt quite uncomfortable..."

"You looked so beautiful, that I could not say anything," David answered candidly.

"Then, just now I am not so beautiful?" inquired she.

"It is not that," he said; "but I was so happy to have this walk alone with you, that..." he stopped short in confusion, and looked at the hillside and the road to Saintes.

"If the walk is any pleasure to you, I am delighted; for I owe you an evening, I think, when you have given up yours for me. When you refused to go to Mme. de Bargeton's, you were quite as generous as Lucien when he made the demand at the risk of vexing her."

"No, not generous, only wise," said David. "And now that we are quite alone under the sky, with no listeners except the bushes and the reeds by the edge of the Charente, let me tell you about my anxiety as to Lucien's present step, dear Eve. After all that I have just said, I hope that you will look on my fears as a refinement of friendship. You and your mother have done all that you could to put him above his social position; but when you stimulated his ambition, did you not unthinkingly condemn him to a hard struggle? How can he maintain himself in the society to which his tastes incline him? I know Lucien; he likes to reap, he does not like toil; it is his nature. Social claims will take up the whole of his time, and for a man who has nothing but his brains, time is capital. He likes to shine; society will stimulate his desires until no money will satisfy them; instead of earning money, he will spend it. You have accustomed him to believe in his great powers, in fact, but the world at large declines to believe in any man's superior intellect until he has achieved some signal success. Now success in literature is only won in solitude and by dogged work. What will Mme. de Bargeton give your brother in return for so many days spent at her feet? Lucien has too much spirit to accept help from her; and he cannot afford, as we know, to cultivate her society, twice ruinous as it is for him. Sooner or later that woman will throw over this dear brother of ours, but not before she has spoiled him for hard work, and given him a taste for luxury and a contempt for our humdrum life. She will develop his love of enjoyment, his inclination for idleness, that debauches a poetic soul. Yes, it makes me tremble to think that this great lady may make a plaything of Lucien. If she cares for him sincerely, he will forget everything else for her; or if she does not love him, she will make him unhappy, for he is wild about her."

"You have sent a chill of dread through my heart," said Eve, stopping as they reached the weir. "But so long as mother is strong enough for her tiring life, so long as I live, we shall earn enough, perhaps, between us to keep Lucien until success comes. My courage will never fail," said Eve, brightening. "There is no hardship in work when we work for one we love; it is not drudgery. It makes me happy to think that I toil so much, if indeed it is toil, for him. Oh, do not be in the least afraid, we will earn money enough to send Lucien into the great world. There lies his road to success."

"And there lies his road to ruin," returned David. "Dear Eve, listen to me. A man needs an independent fortune, or the sublime cynicism of poverty, for the slow execution of great work. Believe me, Lucien's horror of privation is so great, the savor of banquets, the incense of success is so sweet in his nostrils, his self-love has grown so much in Mme. de Bargeton's boudoir, that he will do anything desperate sooner than fall back, and you will never earn enough for his requirements.

"Then you are only a false friend to him!" Eve cried in despair, "or you would not discourage us in this way."

"Eve! Eve!" cried David, "if only I could be a brother to Lucien! You alone can give me that title; he could accept anything from me then; I should claim the right of devoting my life to him with the love that hallows your self-sacrifice, but with some worldly wisdom too. Eve, my darling, give Lucien a store from which he need not blush to draw! His brother's purse will be like his own, will it not? If you only knew all my thoughts about Lucien's position! If he means to go to Mme. de Bargeton's, he must not be my foreman any longer, poor fellow! He ought not to live in L'Houmeau; you ought not to be a working girl; and your mother must give up her employment as well. If you would consent to be my wife, the difficulties will all be smoothed away. Lucien might live on the second floor in the Place du Murier until I can build rooms for him over the shed at the back of the yard (if my father will allow it, that is.). And in that way we would arrange a free and independent life for him. The wish to support Lucien will give me a better will to work than I ever should have had for myself alone; but it rests with you to give me the right to devote myself to him. Some day, perhaps, he will go to Paris, the only place that can bring out all that is in him, and where his talents will be appreciated and rewarded. Living in Paris is expensive, and the earnings of all three of us will be needed for his support. And besides, will not you and your mother need some one to lean upon then? Dear Eve, marry me for love of Lucien; perhaps afterwards you will love me when you see how I shall strive to help him and to make you happy. We are, both of us, equally simple in our tastes; we have few wants; Lucien's welfare shall be the great object of our lives. His heart shall be our treasure-house, we will lay up all our fortune, and think and feel and hope in him."

"Worldly considerations keep us apart," said Eve, moved by this love that tried to explain away its greatness. "You are rich and I am poor. One must love indeed to overcome such a difficulty."

"Then you do not care enough for me?" cried the stricken David.

"But perhaps your father would object..."

"Never mind," said David; "if asking my father is all that is necessary, you will be my wife. Eve, my dear Eve, how you have lightened life for me in a moment; and my heart has been very heavy with thoughts that I could not utter, I did not know how to speak of them. Only tell me that you care for me a little, and I will take courage to tell you the rest."

"Indeed," she said, "you make me quite ashamed; but confidence for confidence, I will tell you this, that I have never thought of any one but you in my life. I looked upon you as one of those men to whom a woman might be proud to belong, and I did not dare to hope so great a thing for myself, a penniless working girl with no prospects."

"That is enough, that is enough," he answered, sitting down on the bar by the weir, for they had gone to and fro like mad creatures over the same length of pathway.

"What is the matter?" she asked, her voice expressing for the first time a woman's sweet anxiety for one who belongs to her.

"Nothing but good," he answered. "It is the sight of a whole lifetime of happiness that dazzles me, as it were; it is overwhelming. Why am I happier than you?" he asked, with a touch of sadness. "For I know that I am happier."

Eve looked at David with mischievous, doubtful eyes that asked an explanation.

"Dear Eve, I am taking more than I give. So I shall always love you more than you love me, because I have more reason to love. You are an angel; I am a man."

"I am not so learned," Eve said, smiling. "I love you..."

"As much as you love Lucien?" he broke in.

"Enough to be your wife, enough to devote myself to you, to try not to add anything to your burdens, for we shall have some struggles; it will not be quite easy at first."

"Dear Eve, have you known that I loved you since the first day I saw you?"

"Where is the woman who does not feel that she is loved?"

"Now let me get rid of your scruples as to my imaginary riches. I am a poor man, dear. Yes, it pleased my father to ruin me; he made a speculation of me, as a good many so-called benefactors do. If I make a fortune, it will be entirely through you. That is not a lover's speech, but sober, serious earnest. I ought to tell you about my faults, for they are exceedingly bad ones in a man who has his way to make. My character and habits and favorite occupations all unfit me for business and money-getting, and yet we can only make money by some kind of industry; if I have some faculty for the discovery of gold-mines, I am singularly ill-adapted for getting the gold out of them. But you who, for your brother's sake, went into the smallest details, with a talent for thrift, and the patient watchfulness of the born man of business, you will reap the harvest that I shall sow. The present state of things, for I have been like one of the family for a long time, weighs so heavily upon me, that I have spent days and nights in search of some way of making a fortune. I know something of chemistry, and a knowledge of commercial requirements has put me on the scent of a discovery that is likely to pay. I can say nothing as yet about it; there will be a long while to wait; perhaps for some years we may have a hard time of it; but I shall find out how to make a commercial article at last. Others are busy making the same researches, and if I am first in the field, we shall have a large fortune. I have said nothing to Lucien, his enthusiastic nature would spoil everything; he would convert my hopes into realities, and begin to live like a lord, and perhaps get into debt. So keep my secret for me. Your sweet and dear companionship will be consolation in itself during the long time of experiment, and the desire to gain wealth for you and Lucien will give me persistence and tenacity..."

"I had guessed this too," Eve said, interrupting him; "I knew that you were one of those inventors, like my poor father, who must have a woman to take care of them."

"Then you love me! Ah! say so without fear to me, who saw a symbol of my love for you in your name. Eve was the one woman in the world; if it was true in the outward world for Adam, it is true again in the inner world of my heart for me. My God! do you love me?"

"Yes," said she, lengthening out the word as if to make it cover the extent of feeling expressed by a single syllable.

"Well, let us sit here," he said, and taking Eve's hand, he went to a great baulk of timber lying below the wheels of a paper-mill. "Let me breathe the evening air, and hear the frogs croak, and watch the moonlight quivering upon the river; let me take all this world about us into my soul, for it seems to me that my happiness is written large over it all; I am seeing it for the first time in all its splendor, lighted up by love, grown fair through you. Eve, dearest, this is the first moment of pure and unmixed joy that fate has given to me! I do not think that Lucien can be as happy as I am."

David felt Eve's hand, damp and quivering in his own, and a tear fell upon it.

"May I not know the secret?" she pleaded coaxingly.

"You have a right to know it, for your father was interested in the matter, and to-day it is a pressing question, and for this reason. Since the downfall of the Empire, calico has come more and more into use, because it is so much cheaper than linen. At the present moment, paper is made of a mixture of hemp and linen rags, but the raw material is dear, and the expense naturally retards the great advance which the French press is bound to make. Now you cannot increase the output of linen rags, a given population gives a pretty constant result, and it only increases with the birth-rate. To make any perceptible difference in the population for this purpose, it would take a quarter of a century and a great revolution in habits of life, trade, and agriculture. And if the supply of linen rags is not enough to meet one-half nor one-third of the demand, some cheaper material than linen rags must be found for cheap paper. This deduction is based on facts that came under my knowledge here. The Angouleme paper-makers, the last to use pure linen rags, say that the proportion of cotton in the pulp has increased to a frightful extent of late years."

In answer to a question from Eve, who did not know what "pulp" meant, David gave an account of paper-making, which will not be out of place in a volume which owes its existence in book form to the paper industry no less than to the printing-press; but the long digression, doubtless, had best be condensed at first.

Paper, an invention not less marvelous than the other dependent invention of printing, was known in ancient times in China. Thence by the unrecognized channels of commerce the art reached Asia Minor, where paper was made of cotton reduced to pulp and boiled. Parchment had become so extremely dear that a cheap substitute was discovered in an imitation of the cotton paper known in the East as *charta bombycina*. The imitation, made from rags, was first made at Basel, in 1170, by a colony of Greek refugees, according to some authorities; or at Padua, in 1301, by an Italian named Pax, according to others. In these ways the manufacture of paper was perfected slowly and in obscurity; but this much is certain, that so early as the reign of Charles VI., paper pulp for playing-cards was made in Paris.

When those immortals, Faust, Coster, and Gutenberg, invented the Book, craftsmen as obscure as many a great artist of those times appropriated paper to the uses of typography. In the fifteenth century, that naive and vigorous age, names were given to the various formats as well as to the different sizes of type, names that bear the impress of the naivete of the times; and the various sheets came to be known by the different watermarks on their centres;

the grapes, the figure of our Saviour, the crown, the shield, or the flower-pot, just as at a later day, the eagle of Napoleon's time gave the name to the "double-eagle" size. And in the same way the types were called Cicero, Saint-Augustine, and Canon type, because they were first used to print the treatises of Cicero and theological and liturgical works. Italics are so called because they were invented in Italy by Aldus of Venice.

Before the invention of machine-made paper, which can be woven in any length, the largest sized sheets were the *grand jesus* and the double columbier (this last being scarcely used now except for atlases or engravings), and the size of paper for printers' use was determined by the dimensions of the impression-stone. When David explained these things to Eve, web-paper was almost undreamed of in France, although, about 1799, Denis Robert d'Essonne had invented a machine for turning out a ribbon of paper, and Didot-Saint-Leger had since tried to perfect it. The vellum paper invented by Ambroise Didot only dates back as far as 1780.

This bird's eye view of the history of the invention shows incontestably that great industrial and intellectual advances are made exceedingly slowly, and little by little, even as Nature herself proceeds. Perhaps articulate speech and the art of writing were gradually developed in the same groping way as typography and paper-making.

"Rag-pickers collect all the rags and old linen of Europe," the printer concluded, "and buy any kind of tissue. The rags are sorted and ware-housed by the wholesale rag merchants, who supply the paper-mills. To give you some idea of the extent of the trade, you must know, mademoiselle, that in 1814 Cardon the banker, owner of the pulping troughs of Bruges and Langlee (where Leorier de l'Isle endeavored in 1776 to solve the very problem that occupied your father), Cardon brought an action against one Proust for an error in weights of two mil-lions in a total of ten million pounds' weight of rags, worth about four million francs! The manufacturer washes the rags and reduces them to a thin pulp, which is strained, exactly as a cook strains sauce through a tamis, through an iron frame with a fine wire bottom where the mark which give its name to the size of the paper is woven. The size of this *mould*, as it is called, regulates the size of the sheet.

"When I was with the Messieurs Didot," David continued, "they were very much interested in this question, and they are still interested; for the improvement which your father endeavored to make is a great commercial requirement, and one of the crying needs of the time. And for this reason: although linen lasts so much longer than cotton, that it is in reality cheaper in the end, the poor would rather make the smaller outlay in the first instance, and, by virtue of the law of *Vae victis!* pay enormously more before they have done. The middle classes do the same. So there is a scarcity of linen. In England, where four-fifths of the population use cotton to the exclusion of linen, they make nothing but cotton paper. The cotton paper is very soft and easily creased to begin with, and it has a further defect: it is so soluble that if you seep a book made of cotton paper in water for fifteen minutes, it turns to a pulp, while an old book left in water for a couple of hours is not spoilt. You could dry the old book, and the pages, though yellow and faded, would still be legible, the work would not be destroyed.

"There is a time coming when legislation will equalize our fortunes, and we shall all be poor together; we shall want our linen and our books to be cheap, just as people are beginning to prefer small pictures because they have not wall space enough for large ones. Well, the shirts and the books will not last, that is all; it is the same on all sides, solidity is drying out. So this problem is one of the first importance for literature, science, and politics.

"One day, in my office, there was a hot discussion going on about the material that the Chinese use for making paper. Their paper is far better than ours, because the raw material is better; and a good deal was said about this thin, light Chinese paper, for if it is light and thin, the texture is close, there are no transparent spots in it. In Paris there are learned men among the printers' readers; Fourier and Pierre Leroux are Lachevardiere's readers at this moment; and the Comte de Saint-Simon, who happened to be correcting proofs for us, came in in the middle of the discussion. He told us at once that, according to Kempfer and du Halde, the Broussonetia furnishes the substance of the Chinese paper; it is a vegetable substance (like linen or cotton for that matter). Another reader maintained that Chinese paper was principally made of an animal substance, to wit, the silk that is abundant there. They made a bet about it in my presence. The Messieurs Didot are printers to the Institute, so naturally they referred the question to that learned body. M. Marcel, who used to be superintendent of the Royal Printing Establishment, was umpire, and he sent the two readers to M. l'Abbe Grozier, Librarian at the Arsenal. By the Abbe's decision they both lost their wages. The paper was not made of silk nor yet from the *Broussonetia*; the pulp proved to be the triturated fibre of some kind of bamboo. The Abbe Grozier had a Chinese book, an iconographical and technological work, with a great many pictures in it, illustrating all the different processes of paper-making, and he showed us a picture of the workshop with the bamboo stalks lying in a heap in the corner; it was extremely well drawn.

"Lucien told me that your father, with the intuition of a man of talent, had a glimmering of a notion of some way of replacing linen rags with an exceedingly common vegetable product, not previously manufactured, but taken direct from the soil, as the Chinese use vegetable fibre at first hand. I have classified the guesses made by those who came before me, and have begun to study the question. The bamboo is a kind of reed; naturally I began to think of the reeds that grow here in France.

"Labor is very cheap in China, where a workman earns three halfpence a day, and this cheapness of labor enables the Chinese to manipulate each sheet of paper separately. They take it out of the mould, and press it between heated tablets of white porcelain, that is the secret of the surface and consistence, the lightness and satin smoothness of the best paper in the world. Well, here in Europe the work must be done by machinery; machinery must take the place of cheap Chinese labor. If we could but succeed in making a cheap paper of as good a quality, the weight and thickness of printed books would be reduced by more than one-half. A set of Voltaire, printed on our woven paper and bound, weighs about two hundred and fifty pounds; it would only weigh fifty if we used Chinese paper. That surely would be a triumph, for the housing of many books has come to be a difficulty; everything has grown smaller of late; this is not an age of giants; men have shrunk, everything about them shrinks, and house-room into the bargain. Great mansions and great suites of rooms will be abolished sooner or later in Paris, for no one will afford to live in the great houses built by our forefathers. What a disgrace for our age if none of its books should last! Dutch paper – that is, paper made from flax – will be quite unobtainable in ten years' time. Well, your brother told me of this idea of your father's, this plan for using vegetable fibre in paper-making, so you see that if I succeed, you have a right to..."

Lucien came up at that moment and interrupted David's generous assertion.

"I do not know whether you have found the evening pleasant," said he; "it has been a cruel time for me."

"Poor Lucien! what can have happened?" cried Eve, as she saw her brother's excited face.

The poet told the history of his agony, pouring out a flood of clamorous thoughts into those friendly hearts, Eve and David listening in pained silence to a torrent of woes that exhibited such greatness and such pettiness.

"M. de Bargeton is an old dotard. The indigestion will carry him off before long, no doubt," Lucien said, as he made an end, "and then I will look down on these proud people; I will marry Mme. de Bargeton. I read to-night in her eyes a love as great as mine for her. Yes, she felt all that I felt; she comforted me; she is as great and noble as she is gracious and beautiful. She will never give me up."

"It is time that life was made smooth for him, is it not?" murmured David, and for answer Eve pressed his arm without speaking. David guessed her thoughts, and began at once to tell Lucien about his own plans.

If Lucien was full of his troubles, the lovers were quite as full of themselves. So absorbed were they, so eager that Lucien should approve their happiness, that neither Eve nor David so much as noticed his start of surprise at the news. Mme. de Bargeton's lover had been dreaming of a great match for his sister; he would reach a high position first, and then secure himself by an alliance with some family of influence, and here was one more obstacle in his way to success! His hopes were dashed to the ground. "If Mme. de Bargeton consents to be Mme. de Rubempre, she would never care to have David Sechard for a brother-in-law!"

This stated clearly and precisely was the thought that tortured Lucien's inmost mind. "Louise is right!" he thought bitterly. "A man with a career before him is never understood by his family."

If the marriage had not been announced immediately after Lucien's fancy had put M. de Bargeton to death, he would have been radiant with heartfelt delight at the news. If he had thought soberly over the probable future of a beautiful and penniless girl like Eve Chardon, he would have seen that this marriage was a piece of unhoped-for good fortune. But he was living just now in a golden dream; he had soared above all barriers on the wings of an *if*; he had seen a vision of himself, rising above society; and it was painful to drop so suddenly down to hard fact.

Eve and David both thought that their brother was overcome with the sense of such generosity; to them, with their noble natures, the silent consent was a sign of true friendship. David began to describe with kindly and cordial eloquence the happy fortunes in store for them all. Unchecked by protests put in by Eve, he furnished his first floor with a lover's lavishness, built a second floor with boyish good faith for Lucien, and rooms above the shed for Mme. Chardon – he meant to be a son to her. In short, he made the whole family so happy and his brother-in-law so independent, that Lucien fell under the spell of David's voice and Eve's caresses; and as they went through the shadows beside the still Charente, a gleam in the warm, star-lit night, he forgot the sharp crown of thorns that had been pressed upon his head. "M. de Rubempre" discovered David's real nature, in fact. His facile character returned almost at once to the innocent, hard-working burgher life that he knew; he saw it transfigured and free from care. The buzz of the aristocratic world grew more and more remote; and when at length they came upon the paved road of L'Houmeau, the ambitious poet grasped his brother's hand, and made a third in the joy of the happy lovers.

"If only your father makes no objection to the marriage," he said.

"You know how much he troubles himself about me; the old man lives for himself," said David. "But I will go over to Marsac to-morrow and see him, if it is only to ask leave to build."

David went back to the house with the brother and sister, and asked Mme. Chardon's consent to his marriage with the eagerness of a man who would fain have no delay. Eve's mother took her daughter's hand, and gladly laid it in David's; and the lover, grown bolder on this, kissed his fair betrothed on the forehead, and she flushed red, and smiled at him.

"The betrothal of the poor," the mother said, raising her eyes as if to pray for heaven's blessing upon them. – "You are brave, my boy," she added, looking at David, "but we have fallen on evil fortune, and I am afraid lest our bad luck should be infectious."

"We shall be rich and happy," David said earnestly. "To begin with, you must not go out nursing any more, and you must come and live with your daughter and Lucien in Angouleme."

The three began at once to tell the astonished mother all their charming plans, and the family party gave themselves up to the pleasure of chatting and weaving a romance, in which it is so pleasant to enjoy future happiness, and to store the unsown harvest. They had to put David out at the door; he could have wished the evening to last for ever, and it was one o'clock in the morning when Lucien and his future brother-in-law reached the Palet Gate. The unwonted movement made honest Postel uneasy; he opened the window, and looking through the Venetian shutters, he saw a light in Eve's room.

"What can be happening at the Chardons'?" thought he, and seeing Lucien come in, he called out to him-

"What is the matter, sonny? Do you want me to do anything?"

"No, sir," returned the poet; "but as you are our friend, I can tell you about it; my mother has just given her consent to my sister's engagement to David Sechard."

For all answer, Postel shut the window with a bang, in despair that he had not asked for Mlle. Chardon earlier.

David, however, did not go back into Angouleme; he took the road to Marsac instead, and walked through the night the whole way to his father's house. He went along by the side of the croft just as the sun rose, and caught sight of the old "bear's" face under an almond-tree that grew out of the hedge.

"Good day, father," called David.

"Why, is it you, my boy? How come you to be out on the road at this time of day? There is your way in," he added, pointing to a little wicket gate. "My vines have flowered and not a shoot has been frosted. There will be twenty puncheons or more to the acre this year; but then look at all the dung that has been put on the land!"

"Father, I have come on important business."

"Very well; how are your presses doing? You must be making heaps of money as big as yourself."

"I shall some day, father, but I am not very well off just now."

"They all tell me that I ought not to put on so much manure," replied his father. "The gentry, that is M. le Marquis, M. le Comte, and Monsieur What-do-you-call-'em, say that I am letting down the quality of the wine. What is the good of book-learning except to muddle your wits? Just you listen: these gentlemen get seven, or sometimes eight puncheons of wine to the acre, and they sell them for sixty francs apiece, that means four hundred francs per acre at most in a good year. Now, I make twenty puncheons, and get thirty francs apiece for them – that is six hundred francs! And where are they, the fools? Quality, quality, what is quality to me? They can keep their quality for themselves, these Lord Marquises. Quality means hard cash for me, that is what it means, You were saying?..."

"I am going to be married, father, and I have come to ask for..."

"Ask me for what? Nothing of the sort, my boy. Marry; I give you my consent, but as for giving you anything else, I haven't a penny to bless myself with. Dressing the soil is the ruin of me. These two years I have been paying money out of pocket for top-dressing, and taxes, and expenses of all kinds; Government eats up everything, nearly all the profit goes to the Government. The poor growers have made nothing these last two seasons. This year things don't look so bad; and, of course, the beggarly puncheons have gone up to eleven francs already. We work to put money into the coopers' pockets. Why, are you going to marry before the vintage?..."

"I only came to ask for your consent, father."

"Oh! that is another thing. And who is the victim, if one may ask?"

"I am going to marry Mlle. Eve Chardon."

"Who may she be? What kind of victual does she eat?"

"She is the daughter of the late M. Chardon, the druggist in L'Houmeau."

"You are going to marry a girl out of L'Houmeau! *you*! a burgess of Angouleme, and printer to His Majesty! This is what comes of book-learning! Send a boy to school, forsooth! Oh! well, then she is very rich, is she, my boy?" and the old vinegrower came up closer with a cajoling manner; "if you are marrying a girl out of L'Houmeau, it must be because she has lots of cash, eh? Good! you will pay me my rent now. There are two years and one-quarter owing, you know, my boy; that is two thousand seven hundred francs altogether; the money will come just in the nick of time to pay the cooper. If it was anybody else, I should have a right to ask for interest; for, after all, business is business, but I will let you off the interest. Well, how much has she?"

"Just as much as my mother had."

The old vinegrower very nearly said, "Then she has only ten thousand francs!" but he recollected just in time that he had declined to give an account of her fortune to her son, and exclaimed, "She has nothing!"

"My mother's fortune was her beauty and intelligence," said David.

"You just go into the market and see what you can get for it! Bless my buttons! what bad luck parents have with their children. David, when I married, I had a paper cap on my head for my whole fortune, and a pair of arms; I was a poor pressman; but with the fine printing-house that I gave you, with your industry, and your education, you might marry a burgess' daughter, a woman with thirty or forty thousand francs. Give up your fancy, and I will find you a wife myself. There is some one about three miles away, a miller's widow, thirty-two years old, with a hundred thousand francs in land. There is your chance! You can add her property to Marsac, for they touch. Ah! what a fine property we should have, and how I would look after it! They say she is going to marry her foreman Courtois, but you are the better man of the two. I would look after the mill, and she should live like a lady up in Angouleme."

"I am engaged, father."

"David, you know nothing of business; you will ruin yourself, I see. Yes, if you marry this girl out of L'Houmeau, I shall square accounts and summons you for the rent, for I see that no good will come of this. Oh! my presses, my poor presses! it took some money to grease you and keep you going. Nothing but a good year can comfort me after this."

"It seems to me, father, that until now I have given you very little trouble..."

"And paid mighty little rent," put in his parent.

"I came to ask you something else besides. Will you build a second floor to your house, and some rooms above the shed?"

"Deuce a bit of it; I have not the cash, and that you know right well. Besides, it would be money thrown clean away, for what would it bring in? Oh! you get up early of a morning to come and ask me to build you a place that would ruin a king, do you? Your name may be David, but I have not got Solomon's treasury. Why, you are mad! or they changed my child at nurse. There is one for you that will have grapes on it," he said, interrupting himself to point out a shoot. "Offspring of this sort don't disappoint their parents; you dung the vines, and they repay you for it. I sent you to school; I spent any amount of money to make a scholar of you; I sent you to the Didots to learn your business; and all this fancy education ends in a daughter-in-law out of L'Houmeau without a penny to her name. If you had not studied books, if I had kept you under my eye, you would have done as I pleased, and you would be marrying a miller's widow this day with a hundred thousand francs in hand, to say nothing of the mill. Oh! your cleverness leads you to imagine that I am going to reward this fine sentiment by building palaces for you, does it? . . . Really, anybody might think that the house that has been a house these two hundred years was nothing but a pigsty, not fit for the girl out of L'Houmeau to sleep in! What next! She is the Queen of France, I suppose."

"Very well, father, I will build the second floor myself; the son will improve his father's property. It is not the usual way, but it happens so sometimes."

"What, my lad! you can find money for building, can you, though you can't find money to pay the rent, eh! You sly dog, to come round your father."

The question thus raised was hard to lay, for the old man was only too delighted to seize an opportunity of posing as a good father without disbursing a penny; and all that David could obtain was his bare consent to the marriage and free leave to do what he liked in the house – at his own expense; the old "bear," that pattern of a thrifty parent, kindly consenting not to demand the rent and drain the savings to which David imprudently owned. David went back again in low spirits. He saw that he could not reckon on his father's help in misfortune.

In Angouleme that day people talked of nothing but the Bishop's epigram and Mme. de Barge-ton's reply. Every least thing that happened that evening was so much exaggerated and embellished and twisted out of all knowledge, that the poet became the hero of the hour. While this storm in a teacup raged on high, a few drops fell among the *bourgeoisie*; young men looked enviously after Lucien as he passed on his way through Beaulieu, and he overheard chance phrases that filled him with conceit.

"There is a lucky young fellow!" said an attorney's clerk, named Petit-Claud, a plain-featured youth who had been at school with Lucien, and treated him with small, patronizing airs.

"Yes, he certainly is," answered one of the young men who had been present on the occasion of the reading; "he is a good-looking fellow, he has some brains, and Mme. de Bargeton is quite wild about him."

Lucien had waited impatiently until he could be sure of finding Louise alone. He had to break the tidings of his sister's marriage to the arbitress of his destinies. Perhaps after yesterday's soiree, Louise would be kinder than usual, and her kindness might lead to a moment of happiness. So he thought, and he was not mistaken; Mme. de Bargeton met him with a vehemence of sentiment that seemed like a touching progress of passion to the novice in love. She abandoned her hands, her beautiful golden hair, to the burning kisses of the poet who had passed through such an ordeal.

"If only you could have seen your face whilst you were reading," cried Louise, using the familiar *tu*, the caress of speech, since yesterday, while her white hands wiped the pearls of sweat from the brows on which she set a poet's crown. "There were sparks of fire in those beautiful eyes! From your lips, as I watched them, there fell the golden chains that suspend the hearts of men upon the poet's mouth. You shall read Chenier through to me from beginning to end; he is the lover's poet. You shall not be unhappy any longer; I will not have it. Yes, dear angel, I will make an oasis for you, there you shall live your poet's life, sometimes busy, sometimes languid; indolent, full of work, and musing by turns; but never forget that you owe your laurels to me, let that thought be my noble guerdon for the sufferings which I must endure. Poor love! the world will not spare me any more than it has spared you; the world is avenged on all happiness in which it has no share. Yes, I shall always be a mark for envy – did you not see that last night? The bloodthirsty insects are quick enough to drain every wound that they pierce. But I was happy; I lived. It is so long since all my heartstrings vibrated."

The tears flowed fast, and for all answer Lucien took Louise's hand and gave it a lingering kiss. Every one about him soothed and caressed the poet's vanity; his mother and his sister and David and Louise now did the same. Every one helped to raise the imaginary pedestal on which he had set himself. His friends's kindness and the fury of his enemies combined to establish him more firmly in an ureal world. A young imagination readily falls in with the flattering estimates of others, a handsome young fellow so full of promise finds others eager to help him on every side, and only after one or two sharp and bitter lessons does he begin to see himself as an ordinary mortal.

"My beautiful Louise, do you mean in very truth to be my Beatrice, a Beatrice who condescends to be loved?"

Louise raised the fine eyes, hitherto down-dropped.

"If you show yourself worthy – some day!" she said, with an angelic smile which belied her words. "Are you not happy? To be the sole possessor of a heart, to speak freely at all times, with the certainty of being understood, is not this happiness?"

"Yes," he answered, with a lover's pout of vexation.

"Child!" she exclaimed, laughing at him. "Come, you have something to tell me, have you not? You came in absorbed in thought, my Lucien."

Lucien, in fear and trembling, confided to his beloved that David was in love with his sister Eve, and that his sister Eve was in love with David, and that the two were to be married shortly.

"Poor Lucien!" said Louise, "he was afraid he should be beaten and scolded, as if it was he himself that was going to be married! Why, where is the harm?" she continued, her fingers toying with Lucien's hair. "What is your family to me when you are an exception? Suppose that my father were to marry his cook, would that trouble you much? Dear boy, lovers are for each other their whole family. Have I a greater interest than my Lucien in the world? Be great, find the way to win fame, that is our affair!"

This selfish answer made Lucien the happiest of mortals. But in the middle of the fantastic reasonings, with which Louise convinced him that they two were alone in the world, in came M. de Bargeton. Lucien frowned and seemed to be taken aback, but Louise made him a sign, and asked him to stay to dinner and to read Andre de Chenier aloud to them until people arrived for their evening game at cards.

"You will give her pleasure," said M. de Bargeton, "and me also. Nothing suits me better than listening to reading aloud after dinner."

Cajoled by M. de Bargeton, cajoled by Louise, waited upon with the respect which servants show to a favored guest of the house, Lucien remained in the Hotel de Bargeton, and began to think of the luxuries which he enjoyed for the time being as the rightful accessories of Lucien de Rubempre. He felt his position so strong through Louise's love and M. de Bargeton's weakness, that as the rooms filled, he assumed a lordly air, which that fair lady encouraged. He tasted the delights of despotic sway which Nais had acquired by right of conquest, and liked to share with him; and, in short, that evening he tried to act up to the part of the lion of the little town. A few of those who marked these airs drew their own conclusions from them, and thought that, according to the old expression, he had come to the last term with the lady. Amelie, who had come with M. du Chatelet, was sure of the deplorable fact, in a corner of the drawing-room, where the jealous and envious gathered together.

"Do not think of calling Nais to account for the vanity of a youngster, who is as proud as he can be because he has got into society, where he never expected to set foot," said Chatelet. "Don't you see that this Chardon takes the civility of a woman of the world for an advance? He does not know the difference between the silence of real passion and the patronizing graciousness due to his good looks and youth and talent. It would be too bad if women were blamed for all the desires which they inspire. *He* certainly is in love with her, but as for Nais..."

"Oh! Nais," echoed the perfidious Amelie, "Nais is well enough pleased. A young man's love has so many attractions – at her age. A woman grows young again in his company; she is a girl, and acts a girl's hesitation and manners, and does not dream that she is ridiculous. Just look! Think of a druggist's son giving himself a conqueror's airs with Mme. de Bargeton."

"Love knows nought of high or low degree," hummed Adrien.

There was not a single house in Angouleme next day where the degree of intimacy between M. Chardon (alias de Rubempre) and Mme. de Bargeton was not discussed; and though the utmost extent of their guilt amounted to two or three kisses, the world already chose to believe the worst of both. Mme. de Bargeton paid the penalty of her sovereignty. Among the various eccentricities of society, have you never noticed its erratic judgments and the unaccountable differences in the standard it requires of this or that man or woman? There are some persons who may do anything; they may behave totally irrationally, anything becomes them, and it is who shall be first to justify their conduct; then, on the other hand, there are those on whom the world is unaccountably severe, they must do everything well, they are not allowed to fail nor to make mistakes, at their peril they do anything foolish; you might compare these last to the much-admired statues which must come down at once from their pedestal if the frost chips off a nose or a finger. They are not permitted to be human; they are required to be for ever divine and for ever impeccable. So one glance exchanged between Mme. de Bargeton and Lucien outweighed twelve years of Zizine's connection with Francis in the social balance; and a squeeze of the hand drew down all the thunders of the Charente upon the lovers.

David had brought a little secret hoard back with him from Paris, and it was this sum that he set aside for the expenses of his marriage and for the building of the second floor in his father's house. His father's house it was; but, after all, was he not working for himself? It would all be his again some day, and his father was sixty-eight years old. So David build a timbered second story for Lucien, so as not to put too great a strain on the old rifted house-walls. He took pleasure in making the rooms where the fair Eve was to spend her life as brave as might be.

It was a time of blithe and unmixed happiness for the friends. Lucien was tired of the shabbiness of provincial life, and weary of the sordid frugality that looked on a five-franc piece as a fortune, but he bore the hardships and the pinching thrift without grumbling. His moody looks had been succeeded by an expression of radiant hope. He saw the star shining above his head, he had dreams of a great time to come, and built the fabric of his good fortune on M. de Bargeton's tomb. M. de Bargeton, troubled with indigestion from time to time, cherished the happy delusion that indigestion after dinner was a complaint to be cured by a hearty supper.

By the beginning of September, Lucien had ceased to be a printer's foreman; he was M. de Rubempre, housed sumptuously in comparison with his late quarters in the tumbledown attic with the dormer-window, where "young Chardon" had lived in L'Houmeau; he was not even a "man of L'Houmeau"; he lived in the heights of Angouleme, and dined four times a week with Mme. de Bargeton. A friendship had grown up between M. de Rubempre and the Bishop, and he went to the palace. His occupations put him upon a level with the highest rank; his name would be one day among the great names of France; and, in truth, as he went to and fro in his apartments, the pretty sitting-room, the charming bedroom, and the tastefully furnished study, he might console himself for the thought that he drew thirty francs every month out of his mother's and sister's hard earnings; for he saw the day approaching when *An Archer of Charles IX.,* the historical romance on which he had been at work for two years, and a volume of verse entitled *Marguerites*, should spread his fame through the world of literature, and bring in money enough to repay them all, his mother and sister and David. So, grown great in his own eyes, and giving ear to the echoes of his name in the future, he could accept present sacrifices with noble assurance; he smiled at his poverty, he relished the sense of these last days of penury.

Eve and David had set Lucien's happiness before their own. They had put off their wedding, for it took some time to paper and paint their rooms, and to buy the furniture, and Lucien's affairs had been settled first. No one who knew Lucien could wonder at their devotion. Lucien was so engaging, he had such winning ways, his impatience and his desires were so graciously expressed, that his cause was always won before he opened his mouth to speak. This unlucky gift of fortune, if it is the salvation of some, is the ruin of many more. Lucien and his like find a world predisposed in favor of youth and good looks, and ready to protect those who give it pleasure with the selfish good-nature that flings alms to a beggar, if he appeals to the feelings and awakens emotion; and in this favor many a grown child is content to bask instead of putting it to a profitable use. With mistaken notions as to the significance and the motive of social relations they imagine that they shall always meet with deceptive smiles; and so at last the moment comes for them when the world leaves them bald, stripped bare, without fortune or worth, like an elderly coquette by the door of a salon, or a stray rag in the gutter.

Eve herself had wished for the delay. She meant to establish the little household on the most economical footing, and to buy only strict necessaries; but what could two lovers refuse to a brother who watched his sister at her work, and said in tones that came from the heart, "How I wish I could sew!" The sober, observant David had shared in the devotion; and yet, since Lucien's triumph, David had watched him with misgivings; he was afraid that Lucien would change towards them, afraid that he would look down upon their homely ways. Once or twice, to try his brother, David had made him choose between home pleasures and the great world, and saw that Lucien gave up the delights of vanity for them, and exclaimed to himself, "They will not spoil him for us!" Now and again the three friends and Mme. Chardon arranged picnic parties in provincial fashion – a walk in the woods along the Charente, not far from Angouleme, and dinner out on the grass, David's apprentice bringing the basket of provisions to some place appointed before-hand; and at night they would come back, tired somewhat, but the whole excursion had not cost three francs. On great occasion, when they dined at a *restaurat*, as it is called, a sort of a country inn, a compromise between a provincial wineshop and a Parisian *guinguette*, they would spend as much as five francs, divided between David and the Chardons. David gave his brother infinite credit for forsaking Mme. de Bargeton and grand dinners for these days in the country, and the whole party made much of the great man of Angouleme.

Matters had gone so far, that the new home was very nearly ready, and David had gone over to Marsac to persuade his father to come to the wedding, not without a hope that the old man might relent at the sight of his daughter-in-law, and give something towards the heavy expenses of the alterations, when there befell one of those events which entirely change the face of things in a small town.

Lucien and Louise had a spy in Chatelet, a spy who watched, with the persistence of a hate in which avarice and passion are blended, for an opportunity of making a scandal. Sixte meant that Mme. de Bargeton should compromise herself with Lucien in such a way that she should be "lost," as the saying goes; so he posed as Mme. de Bargeton's humble confidant, admired Lucien in the Rue du Minage, and pulled him to pieces everywhere else. Nais had gradually given him *les petites entrees*, in the language of the court, for the lady no longer mistrusted her elderly admirer; but Chatelet had taken too much for granted – love was still in the Platonic stage, to the great despair of Louise and Lucien.

There are, for that matter, love affairs which start with a good or a bad beginning, as you prefer to take it. Two creatures launch into the tactics of sentiment; they talk when they should be acting, and skirmish in the open instead of settling down to a siege. And so they grow tired of one another, expend their longings in empty space; and, having time for reflection, come to their own conclusions about each other. Many a passion that has taken the field in gorgeous array, with colors flying and an ardor fit to turn the world upside down, has turned home again without a victory, inglorious and crestfallen, cutting but a foolish figure after these vain alarums and excursions. Such mishaps are sometimes due to the diffidence of youth, sometimes to the demurs of an inexperienced woman, for old players at this game seldom end in a fiasco of this kind.

Provincial life, moreover, is singularly well calculated to keep desire unsatisfied and maintain a lover's arguments on the intellectual plane, while, at the same time, the very obstacles placed in the way of the sweet intercourse which binds lovers so closely each to each, hurry ardent souls on towards extreme measures. A system of espionage of the most minute and intricate kind underlies provincial life; every house is transparent, the solace of close friendships which break no moral law is scarcely allowed; and such outrageously scandalous constructions are put upon the most innocent human intercourse, that many a woman's character is taken away without cause. One here and there, weighed down by her unmerited punishment, will regret that she has never known to the full the forbidden felicity for which she is suffering. The world, which blames and criticises with a superficial knowledge of the patent facts in which a long inward struggle ends, is in reality a prime agent in bringing such scandals about; and those whose voices are loudest in condemnation of the alleged misconduct of some slandered woman never give a thought to the immediate provocation of the overt step. That step many a woman only takes after she has been unjustly accused and condemned, and Mme. de Bargeton was now on the verge of this anomalous position.

The obstacles at the outset of a passion of this kind are alarming to inexperience, and those in the way of the two lovers were very like the bonds by which the population of Lilliput throttled Gulliver, a multiplicity of nothings, which made all movement impossible, and baffle the most vehement desires. Mme. de Bargeton, for instance, must always be visible. If she had denied herself to visitors when Lucien was with her, it would have been all over with her; she might as well have run away with him at once. It is true that they sat in the boudoir, now grown so familiar to Lucien that he felt as if he had a right to be there; but the doors stood scrupulously open, and everything was arranged with the utmost propriety. M. de Bargeton pervaded the house like a cockchafer; it never entered his head that his wife could wish to be alone with Lucien. If he had been the only person in the way, Nais could have got rid of him, sent him out of the house, or given him something to do; but he was not the only one; visitors flocked in upon her, and so much the more as curiosity increased, for your provincial has a natural bent for teasing, and delights to thwart a growing passion. The servants came and went about the house promiscuously and without a summons; they had formed the habits with a mistress who had nothing to conceal; any change now made in her household ways was tantamount to a confession, and Angouleme still hung in doubt.

Mme. de Bargeton could not set foot outside her house but the whole town knew whither she was going. To take a walk alone with Lucien out of Angouleme would have been a decided measure, indeed; it would have been less dangerous to shut herself up with him in the house. There would have been comments the next day if Lucien had stayed on till midnight after the rooms were emptied. Within as without her house, Mme. de Bargeton lived in public.

These details describe life in the provinces; an intrigue is either openly avoided or impossible anywhere.

Like all women carried away for the first time by passion, Louise discovered the difficulties of her position one by one. They frightened her, and her terror reacted upon the fond talk that fills the fairest hours which lovers spend alone together. Mme. de Bargeton had no country house whither she could take her beloved poet, after the manner of some women who will forge ingenious pretexts for burying themselves in the wilderness; but, weary of living in public, and pushed to extremities by a tyranny which afforded no pleasures sweet enough to compensate for the heaviness of the yoke, she even thought of Escarbas, and of going to see her aged father – so much irritated was she by these paltry obstacles.

Chatelet did not believe in such innocence. He lay in wait, and watched Lucien into the house, and followed a few minutes later, always taking M. de Chandour, the most indiscreet person in the clique, along with him; and, putting that gentleman first, hoped to find a surprise by such perseverance in pursuit of the chance. His own part was a very difficult one to play, and its success was the more doubtful because he was bound to appear neutral if he was to prompt the other actors who were to play in his drama. So, to give himself a countenance, he had attached himself to the jealous Amelie, the better to lull suspicion in Lucien and in Mme. de Bargeton, who was not without perspicacity. In order to spy upon the pair, he had contrived of late to

open up a stock controversy on the point with
M. de Chandour. Chatelet said that Mme. de
Bargeton was simply amusing herself with
Lucien; she was too proud, too high-born, to
stoop to the apothecary's son. The role of
incredulity was in accordance with the plan which
he had laid down, for he wished to appear as
Mme. de Bargeton's champion. Stanislas de
Chandour held that Mme. de Bargeton had not
been cruel to her lover, and Amelie goaded them
to argument, for she longed to know the truth.
Each stated his case, and (as not unfrequently
happens in small country towns) some intimate
friends of the house dropped in in the middle of
the argument. Stanislas and Chatelet vied with
each other in backing up their opinions by
observations extremely pertinent. It was hardly
to be expected that the champions should not
seek to enlist partisans. "What do you yourself
think?" they asked, each of his neighbor. These
polemics kept Mme. de Bargeton and Lucien well
in sight.

At length one day Chatelet called attention to
the fact that whenever he went with M. de
Chandour to Mme. de Bargeton's and found
Lucien there, there was not a sign nor a trace
of anything suspicious; the boudoir door stood
open, the servants came and went, there was
nothing mysterious to betray the sweet crime of
love, and so forth and so forth. Stanislas, who
did not lack a certain spice of stupidity in his
composition, vowed that he would cross the room

on tiptoe the next day, and the perfidious Amelie held him to his bargain.

For Lucien that morrow was the day on which a young man tugs out some of the hairs of his head, and inwardly vows that he will give up the foolish business of sighing. He was accustomed to his situation. The poet, who had seated himself so bashfully in the boudoir-sanctuary of the queen of Angouleme, had been transformed into an urgent lover. Six months had been enough to bring him on a level with Louise, and now he would fain be her lord and master. He left home with a settled determination to be extravagant in his behavior; he would say that it was a matter of life or death to him; he would bring all the resources of torrid eloquence into play; he would cry that he had lost his head, that he could not think, could not write a line. The horror that some women feel for premeditation does honor to their delicacy; they would rather surrender upon the impulse of passion, than in fulfilment of a contract. In general, prescribed happiness is not the kind that any of us desire.

Mme. de Bargeton read fixed purpose in Lucien's eyes and forehead, and in the agitation in his face and manner, and proposed to herself to baffle him, urged thereto partly by a spirit of contradiction, partly also by an exalted conception of love. Being given to exaggeration, she set an exaggerated value upon her person. She looked upon herself as a sovereign lady, a

Beatrice, a Laura. She enthroned herself, like some dame of the Middle Ages, upon a dais, looking down upon the tourney of literature, and meant that Lucien, as in duty bound, should win her by his prowess in the field; he must eclipse "the sublime child," and Lamartine, and Sir Walter Scott, and Byron. The noble creature regarded her love as a stimulating power; the desire which she had kindled in Lucien should give him the energy to win glory for himself. This feminine Quixotry is a sentiment which hallows love and turns it to worthy uses; it exalts and reverences love. Mme. de Bargeton having made up her mind to play the part of Dulcinea in Lucien's life for seven or eight years to come, desired, like many other provincials, to give herself as the reward of prolonged service, a trial of constancy which should give her time to judge her lover.

Lucien began the strife by a piece of vehement petulence, at which a woman laughs so long as she is heart-free, and saddens only when she loves; whereupon Louise took a lofty tone, and began one of her long orations, interlarded with high-sounding words.

"Was that your promise to me, Lucien?" she said, as she made an end. "Do not sow regrets in the present time, so sweet as it is, to poison my after life. Do not spoil the future, and, I say it with pride, do not spoil the present! Is not my whole heart yours? What more must you have?

Can it be that your love is influenced by the clamor of the senses, when it is the noblest privilege of the beloved to silence them? For whom do you take me? Am I not your Beatrice? If I am not something more than a woman for you, I am less than a woman."

"That is just what you might say to a man if you cared nothing at all for him," cried Lucien, frantic with passion.

"If you cannot feel all the sincere love underlying my ideas, you will never be worthy of me."

"You are throwing doubts on my love to dispense yourself from responding to it," cried Lucien, and he flung himself weeping at her feet.

The poor boy cried in earnest at the prospect of remaining so long at the gate of paradise. The tears of the poet, who feels that he is humbled through his strength, were mingled with childish crying for a plaything.

"You have never loved me!" he cried.

"You do not believe what you say," she answered, flattered by his violence.

"Then give me proof that you are mine," said the disheveled poet.

Just at that moment Stanislas came up unheard by either of the pair. He beheld Lucien in tears, half reclining on the floor, with his head on Louise's knee. The attitude was suspicious enough to satisfy Stanislas; he turned sharply round upon Chatelet, who stood at the door of the salon. Mme. de Bargeton sprang up in a moment, but the spies beat a precipate retreat like intruders, and she was not quick enough for them.

"Who came just now?" she asked the servants.

"M. de Chandour and M. du Chatelet," said Gentil, her old footman.

Mme. de Bargeton went back, pale and trembling, to her boudoir.

"If they saw you just now, I am lost," she told Lucien.

"So much the better!" exclaimed the poet, and she smiled to hear the cry, so full of selfish love.

A story of this kind is aggravated in the provinces by the way in which it is told. Everybody knew in a moment that Lucien had been detected at Nais feet. M. de Chandour, elated by the important part he played in the affair, went first to tell the great news at the club, and thence from house to house, Chatelet hastening to say that *he* had seen nothing; but by putting himself out of court, he egged Stanislas on to talk, he drew him on to add fresh details; and Stanislas, thinking himself very witty, added a little to the tale every time that he told it. Every one flocked to Amelie's house that evening, for by that time the most exaggerated versions of the story were in circulation among the Angouleme nobility, every narrator having followed Stanislas' example. Women and men were alike impatient to know the truth; and the women who put their hands before their faces and shrieked the loudest were none other than Mesdames Amelie, Zephirine, Fifine, and Lolotte, all with more or less heavy indictments of illicit love laid to their charge. There were variations in every key upon the painful theme.

"Well, well," said one of the ladies, "poor Nais! have you heard about it? I do not believe it myself; she has a whole blameless record behind her; she is far too proud to be anything but a patroness to M. Chardon. Still, if it is true, I pity her with all my heart."

"She is all the more to be pitied because she is making herself frightfully ridiculous; she is old enough to be M. Lulu's mother, as Jacques called him. The little poet it twenty-two at most; and Nais, between ourselves, is quite forty."

"For my own part," said M. du Chatelet, "I think that M. de Rubempre's position in itself proves Nais' innocence. A man does not go down on his knees to ask for what he has had already."

"That is as may be!" said Francis, with levity that brought Zephirine's disapproving glance down on him.

"Do just tell us how it really was," they besought Stanislas, and formed a small, secret committee in a corner of the salon.

Stanislas, in the long length, had put together a little story full of facetious suggestions, and accompanied it with pantomime, which made the thing prodigiously worse.

"It is incredible!"

"At midday?"

"Nais was the last person whom I should have suspected!"

"What will she do now?"

Then followed more comments, and suppositions without end. Chatelet took Mme. de Bargeton's part; but he defended her so ill, that he stirred the fire of gossip instead of putting it out.

Lili, disconsolate over the fall of the fairest angel in the Angoumoisin hierarchy, went, dissolved in tears, to carry the news to the palace. When the delighted Chatelet was convinced that the whole town was agog, he went off to Mme. de Bargeton's, where, alas! there was but one game of whist that night, and diplomatically asked Nais for a little talk in the boudoir. They sat down on the sofa, and Chatelet began in an undertone-

"You know what Angouleme is talking about, of course?"

"No."

"Very well, I am too much your friend to leave you in ignorance. I am bound to put you in a position to silence slanders, invented, no doubt, by Amelie, who has the overweening audacity to regard herself as your rival. I came to call on you this morning with that monkey of a Stanislas; he was a few paces ahead of me, and he came so far" (pointing to the door of the boudoir); he says that he *saw* you and M. de Rubempre in such a position that he could not enter; he turned round upon me, quite bewildered as I was, and hurried me away before I had time to think; we were out in Beaulieu before he told me why he had beaten a retreat. If I had known, I would not have stirred out of the house till I had cleared up the matter and exonerated you, but it would have proved nothing to go back again then.

"Now, whether Stanislas' eyes deceived him, or whether he is right, *he must have made a mistake*. Dear Nais, do not let that dolt trifle with your life, your honor, your future; stop his mouth at once. You know my position here. I have need of all these people, but still I am entirely yours. Dispose of a life that belongs to you. You have rejected my prayers, but my heart is always yours; I am ready to prove my love for you at any time and in any way. Yes, I will watch over you like a faithful servant, for no reward, but simply for the sake of the pleasure that it is to me to do anything for you, even if you do not know of it. This morning I have said everywhere that I was at the door of the salon, and had seen nothing. If you are asked to give the name of the person who told you about this gossip, pray make use of me. I should be very proud to be your acknowledged champion; but, between ourselves, M. de Bargeton is the proper person to ask Stanislas for an explanation. . . . Suppose that young Rubempre had behaved foolishly, a woman's character ought not to be at the mercy of the first hare-brained boy who flings himself at her feet. That is what I have been saying."

Nais bowed in acknowledgment, and looked thoughtful. She was weary to disgust of provincial life. Chatelet had scarcely begun before her mind turned to Paris. Meanwhile Mme. de Bargeton's adorer found the silence somewhat awkward.

"Dispose of me, I repeat," he added.

"Thank you," answered the lady.

"What do you think of doing?"

"I shall see."

A prolonged pause.

"Are you so fond of that young Rubempre?"

A proud smile stole over her lips, she folded her arms, and fixed her gaze on the curtains. Chatelet went out; he could not read that high heart.

Later in the evening, when Lucien had taken his leave, and likewise the four old gentlemen who came for their whist, without troubling themselves about ill-founded tittle-tattle, M. de Bargeton was preparing to go to bed, and had opened his mouth to bid his wife good-night, when she stopped him.

"Come here, dear, I have something to say to you," she said, with a certain solemnity.

M. de Bargeton followed her into the boudoir.

"Perhaps I have done wrongly," she said, "to show a warm interest in M. de Rubempre, which he, as well as the stupid people here in the town, has misinterpreted. This morning Lucien threw himself here at my feet with a declaration, and Stanislas happened to come in just as I told the boy to get up again. A woman, under any circumstances, has claims which courtesy prescribes to a gentleman; but in contempt of these, Stanislas has been saying that he came unexpectedly and found us in an equivocal position. I was treating the boy as he deserved. If the young scatterbrain knew of the scandal caused by his folly, he would go, I am convinced, to insult Stanislas, and compel him to fight. That would simply be a public proclamation of his love. I need not tell you that your wife is pure; but if you think, you will see that it is something dishonoring for both you and me if M. de Rubempre defends her. Go at once to Stanislas and ask him to give you satisfaction for his insulting language; and mind, you must not accept any explanation short of a full and public retraction in the presence of witnesses of credit. In this way you will win back the respect of all right-minded people; you will behave like a man of spirit and a gentleman, and you will have a right to my esteem. I shall send Gentil on horseback to the Escarbas; my father must be your second; old as he is, I know that he is the man to trample this puppet under foot that has smirched the reputation of a Negrepelisse. You have the choice of weapons, choose pistols; you are an admirable shot."

"I am going," said M. de Bargeton, and he took his hat and his walking cane.

"Good, that is how I like a man to behave, dear; you are a gentleman," said his wife. She felt touched by his conduct, and made the old man very happy and proud by putting up her forehead for a kiss. She felt something like a maternal affection for the great child; and when the carriage gateway had shut with a clang behind him, the tears came into her eyes in spite of herself.

"How he loves me!" she thought. "He clings to life, poor, dear man, and yet he would give his life for me."

It did not trouble M. de Bargeton that he must stand up and face his man on the morrow, and look coolly into the muzzle of a pistol pointed straight at him; no, only one thing in the business made him feel uncomfortable, and on the way to M. de Chandour's house he quaked inwardly.

"What shall I say?" he thought within himself; "Nais really ought to have told me what to say," and the good gentleman racked his brains to compose a speech that should not be ridiculous.

But people of M. de Bargeton's stamp, who live perforce in silence because their capacity is limited and their outlook circumscribed, often behave at great crises with a ready-made solemnity. If they say little, it naturally follows that they say little that is foolish; their extreme lack of confidence leads them to think a good deal over the remarks that they are obliged to make; and, like Balaam's ass, they speak marvelously to the point if a miracle loosens their tongues. So M. de Bargeton bore himself like a man of uncommon sense and spirit, and justified the opinion of those who held that he was a philosopher of the school of Pythagoras.

He reached Stanislas' house at nine o'clock, bowed silently to Amelie before a whole room full of people, and greeted others in turn with that simple smile of his, which under the present circumstances seemed profoundly ironical. There followed a great silence, like the pause before a storm. Chatelet had made his way back again, and now looked in a very significant fashion from M. de Bargeton to Stanislas, whom the injured gentleman accosted politely.

Chatelet knew what a visit meant at this time of night, when old M. de Bargeton was invariably in his bed. It was evidently Nais who had set the feeble arm in motion. Chatelet was on such a footing in that house that he had some right to interfere in family concerns. He rose to his feet and took M. de Bargeton aside, saying, "Do you wish to speak to Stanislas?"

"Yes," said the old gentleman, well pleased to find a go-between who perhaps might say his say for him.

"Very well; go into Amelie's bedroom," said the controller of excise, likewise well pleased at the prospect of a duel which possibly might make Mme. de Bargeton a widow, while it put a bar between her and Lucien, the cause of the quarrel. Then Chatelet went to M. de Chandour.

"Stanislas," he said, "here comes Bargeton to call you to account, no doubt, for the things you have been saying about Nais. Go into your wife's room, and behave, both of you, like gentlemen. Keep the thing quiet, and make a great show of politeness, behave with phlegmatic British dignity, in short."

In another minute Stanislas and Chatelet went to Bargeton.

"Sir," said the injured husband, "do you say that you discovered Mme. de Bargeton and M. de Rubempre in an equivocal position?"

"M. Chardon," corrected Stanislas, with ironical stress; he did not take Bargeton seriously.

"So be it," answered the other. "If you do not withdraw your assertions at once before the company now in your house, I must ask you to look for a second. My father-in-law, M. de

Negrepelisse, will wait upon you at four o'clock to-morrow morning. Both of us may as well make our final arrangements, for the only way out of the affair is the one that I have indicated. I choose pistols, as the insulted party."

This was the speech that M. de Bargeton had ruminated on the way; it was the longest that he had ever made in life. He brought it out without excitement or vehemence, in the simplest way in the world. Stanislas turned pale. "After all, what did I see?" said he to himself.

Put between the shame of eating his words before the whole town, and fear, that caught him by the throat with burning fingers; confronted by this mute personage, who seemed in no humor to stand nonsense, Stanislas chose the more remote peril.

"All right. To-morrow morning," he said, thinking that the matter might be arranged somehow or other.

The three went back to the room. Everybody scanned their faces as they came in; Chatelet was smiling, M. de Bargeton looked exactly as if he were in his own house, but Stanislas looked ghastly pale. At the sight of his face, some of the women here and there guessed the nature of the conference, and the whisper, "They are going to fight!" circulated from ear to ear. One-half of the room was of the opinion that

Stanislas was in the wrong, his white face and his demeanor convicted him of a lie; the other half admired M. de Bargeton's attitude. Chatelet was solemn and mysterious. M. de Bargeton stayed a few minutes, scrutinized people's faces, and retired.

"Have you pistols?" Chatelet asked in a whisper of Stanislas, who shook from head to foot.

Amelie knew what it all meant. She felt ill, and the women flocked about her to take her into her bedroom. There was a terrific sensation; everybody talked at once. The men stopped in the drawing-room, and declared, with one voice, that M. de Bargeton was within his right.

"Would you have thought the old fogy capable of acting like this?" asked M. de Saintot.

"But he was a crack shot when he was young," said the pitiless Jacques. "My father often used to tell me of Bargeton's exploits."

"Pooh! Put them at twenty paces, and they will miss each other if you give them cavalry pistols," said Francis, addressing Chatelet.

Chatelet stayed after the rest had gone to reassure Stanislas and his wife, and to explain that all would go off well. In a duel between a man of sixty and a man of thirty-five, all the advantage lay with the latter.

Early next morning, as Lucien sat at breakfast with David, who had come back alone from Marsac, in came Mme. Chardon with a scared face.

"Well, Lucien," she said, "have you heard the news? Everyone is talking of it, even the people in the market. M. de Bargeton all but killed M. de Chandour this morning in M. Tulloy's meadow; people are making puns on the name. (Tue Poie.) It seems that M. de Chandour said that he found you with Mme. de Bargeton yesterday."

"It is a lie! Mme. de Bargeton is innocent," cried Lucien.

"I heard about the duel from a countryman, who saw it all from his cart. M. de Negrepelisse came over at three o'clock in the morning to be M. de Bargeton's second; he told M. de Chandour that if anything happened to his son-in-law, he should avenge him. A cavalry officer lent the pistols. M. de Negrepelisse tried them over and over again. M. du Chatelet tried to prevent them from practising with the pistols, but they referred the question to the officer; and he said that, unless they meant to behave like children, they ought to have pistols in working order. The seconds put them at twenty-five paces. M. de Bargeton looked as if he had just come out for a walk. He was the first to fire; the ball lodged in M. de Chandour's neck, and he dropped before he could return the shot. The house-surgeon at the hospital has just said that M. de Chandour will have a wry neck for the rest of his days. I came to tell you how it ended, lest you should go to Mme. de Bargeton's or show yourself in Angouleme, for some of M. de Chandour's friends might call you out."

As she spoke, the apprentice brought in Gentil, M. de Bargeton's footman. The man had come with a note for Lucien; it was from Louise.

"You have doubtless heard the news," she wrote, "of the duel between Chandour and my husband. We shall not be at home to any one to-day. Be careful; do not show yourself. I ask this in the name of the affection you bear me. Do you not think that it would be best to spend this melancholy day in listening to your Beatrice, whose whole life has been changed by this event, who has a thousand things to say to you?"

"Luckily, my marriage is fixed for the day after to-morrow," said David, "and you will have an excuse for not going to see Mme. de Bargeton quite so often."

"Dear David," returned Lucien, "she asks me to go to her to-day; and I ought to do as she wishes, I think; she knows better than we do how I should act in the present state of things."

"Then is everything ready here?" asked Mme. Chardon.

"Come and see," cried David, delighted to exhibit the transformation of the first floor. Everything there was new and fresh; everything was pervaded by the sweet influences of early married days, still crowned by the wreath of orange blossoms and the bridal veil; days when the springtide of love finds its reflection in material things, and everything is white and spotless and has not lost its bloom.

"Eve's home will be fit for a princess," said the mother, "but you have spent too much, you have been reckless."

David smiled by way of answer. But Mme. Chardon had touched the sore spot in a hidden wound which caused the poor lover cruel pangs. The cost of carrying out his ideas had far exceeded his estimates; he could not afford to build above the shed. His mother-in-law must wait awhile for the home he had meant to make for her. There is nothing more keenly painful to a generous nature than a failure to keep such promises as these; it is like mortification to the little vanities of affection, as they may be styled. David sedulously hid his embarrassment to spare Lucien; he was afraid that Lucien might be overwhelmed by the sacrifices made for his sake.

"Eve and her girl friends have been working very hard, too," said Mme. Chardon. "The wedding clothes and the house linen are all ready. The girls are so fond of her, that, without letting her

know about it, they have covered the mat-
tresses with white twill and a rose-colored
piping at the edges. So pretty! It makes one
wish one were going to be married."

Mother and daughter had spent all their little
savings to furnish David's home with the
things of which a young bachelor never
thinks. They knew that he was furnishing with
great splendor, for something had been said
about ordering a dinner-service from Limoges,
and the two women had striven to make
Eve's contributions to the housekeeping worthy of David's. This little emulation in love
and generosity could but bring the husband
and wife into difficulties at the very outset
of their married life, with every sign of
homely comfort about them, comfort that
might be regarded as positive luxury in a
place so behind the times as the Angouleme
of those days.

As soon as Lucien saw his mother and David
enter the bedroom with the blue-and-white
draperies and neat furniture that he knew,
he slipped away to Mme. de Bargeton. He
found Nais at table with her husband; M. de
Bargeton's early morning walk had sharpened
his appetite, and he was breakfasting quite
unconcernedly after all that had passed. Lucien saw the dignified face of M. de Negrepelisse, the old provincial noble, a relic of
the old French *noblesse*, sitting beside Nais.

When Gentil announced M. de Rubempre, the white-headed old man gave him a keen, curious glance; the father was anxious to form his own opinions of this man whom his daughter had singled out for notice. Lucien's extreme beauty made such a vivid impression upon him, that he could not repress an approving glance; but at the same time he seemed to regard the affair as a flirtation, a mere passing fancy on his daughter's part. Breakfast over, Louise could leave her father and M. de Bargeton together; she beckoned Lucien to follow her as she withdrew.

"Dear," she said, and the tones of her voice were half glad, half melancholy, "I am going to Paris, and my father is taking Bargeton back with him to the Escarbas, where he will stay during my absence. Mme. d'Espard (she was a Blamont-Chauvry before her marriage) has great influence herself, and influential relations. The d'Espards are connections of ours; they are the older branch of the Negrepelisses; and if she vouchsafes to acknowledge the relationship, I intend to cultivate her a good deal; she may perhaps procure a place for Bargeton. At my solicitation, it might be desired at Court that he should represent the Charente, and that would be a step towards his election here. If he were a deputy, it would further other steps that I wish to take in Paris. You, my darling, have brought about this change in my life. After this morning's duel, I am obliged to shut up my house for some time; for there will be people who will side with the Chandours against us. In our position, and in a small town, absence is the only way of softening down bad feeling. But I shall either succeed, and never see Angouleme again, or I shall not succeed, and then I mean to wait in Paris until the time comes when I can spend my summers at the Escarbas and the winters in Paris. It is the only life for a woman of quality, and I have waited too long before entering upon it. The one day will be enough for our preparations; to-morrow night I shall set out, and you are coming with me, are you not? You shall start first. I will overtake you between Mansle and Ruffec, and we shall soon be in Paris. There, beloved, is the life for a man who has anything in him. We are only at our ease among our equals; we are uncomfortable in any other society. Paris, besides, is the capital of the intellectual world, the stage on which you will succeed; overleap the gulf that separates us quickly. You must not allow your ideas to grow rancid in the provinces; put yourself into communication at once with the great men who represent the nineteenth century. Try to stand well with the Court and with those in power. No honor, no distinction, comes to seek out the talent that perishes for lack of light in a little town; tell me, if you can, the name of any great work of art executed in the provinces! On the contrary, see how Jean-Jacques, himself sublime in his poverty, felt the irresistible attraction of that sun of the intellectual world, which produces ever-new glories and stimulates the intellect – Paris, where men rub against one another. What is it but your duty to hasten to take your place in the succession of pleiades that rise from generation to generation? You have no idea how it contributes to the success of a clever young man to be brought into a high light, socially speaking. I will introduce you to Mme. d'Espard; it is not easy to get into her set; but you meet all the greatest people at her house, Cabinet ministers and ambassadors, and great orators from the Chamber of Deputies, and peers and men of influence, and wealthy or famous people. A young man with good looks and more than sufficient genius could fail to excite interest only by very bad management.

"There is no pettiness about those who are truly great; they will lend you their support; and when you yourself have a high position, your work will rise immensely in public opinion. The great problem for the artist is the problem of putting himself in evidence. In these ways there will be hundreds of chances of making your way, of sinecures, of a pension from the civil list. The Bourbons are so fond of encouraging letters and the arts, and you therefore must be a religious poet and a Royalist poet at the same time. Not only is it the right course, but it is the way to get on in life. Do the Liberals and the Opposition give places and rewards, and make the fortunes of men of letters? Take the right road and reach the goal of genius. You have my secret, do not breathe a syllable of it, and prepare to follow me. – Would you rather not go?" she added, surprised that her lover made no answer.

To Lucien, listening to the alluring words, and bewildered by the rapid bird's-eye view of Paris which they brought before him, it seemed as if hitherto he had been using only half his brain and suddenly had found the other half, so swiftly his ideas widened. He saw himself stagnating in Angouleme like a frog under a stone in a marsh. Paris and her splendors rose before him; Paris, the Eldorado of provincial imaginings, with golden robes and the royal diadem about her brows, and arms out-stretched to talent of every kind. Great men would greet him there as one of their order. Everything smiled upon genius. There, there were no jealous booby-squires to invent stinging gibes and humiliate a man of letters; there was no stupid indifference to poetry in Paris. Paris was the fountain-head of poetry; there the poet was brought into the light and paid for his work. Publishers should no sooner read the opening pages of *An Archer of Charles IX.* than they should open their cash-boxes with "How much do you want?" And besides all this, he understood that this journey with Mme. de Bargeton would virtually give her to him; that they should live together.

So at the words, "Would you rather not go?" tears came into his eyes, he flung his arms about Louise, held her tightly to his heart, and marbled her throat with impassioned kisses. Suddenly he checked himself, as if memory had dealt him a blow.

"Great heavens!" he cried, "my sister is to be married on the day after to-morrow!"

That exclamation was the last expiring cry of noble and single-hearted boyhood. The so-powerful ties that bind young hearts to home, and a first friendship, and all early affections, were to be severed at one ruthless blow.

"Well," cried the haughty Negrepelisse, "and what has your sister's marriage to do with the progress of our love? Have you set your mind so much on being best man at a wedding party of tradespeople and workingmen, that you cannot give up these exalted joys for my sake? A great sacrifice, indeed!" she went on, scornfully. "This morning I sent my husband out to fight in your quarrel. There, sir, go; I am mistaken in you."

She sank fainting upon the sofa. Lucien went to her, entreating her pardon, calling execrations upon his family, his sister, and David.

"I had such faith in you!" she said. "M. de Cante-Croix had an adored mother; but to win a letter from me, and the words, 'I am satisfied,' he fell in the thick of the fight. And now, when I ask you to take a journey with me, you cannot think of giving up a wedding dinner for my sake."

Lucien was ready to kill himself; his desperation was so unfeigned, that Louise forgave him, though at the same time she made him feel that he must redeem his mistake.

"Come, come," she said, "be discreet, and to-morrow at midnight be upon the road, a hundred paces out of Mansle."

Lucien felt the globe shrink under his feet; he went back to David's house, hopes pursuing him as the Furies followed Orestes, for he had glimmerings of endless difficulties, all summed up in the appalling words, "Where is the money to come from?"

He stood in such terror of David's perspicacity, that he locked himself into his pretty new study until he could recover himself, his head was swimming in this new position. So he must leave the rooms just furnished for him at such a cost, and all the sacrifices that had been made for him had been made in vain. Then it occurred to Lucien that his mother might take the rooms and save David the heavy expense of building at the end of the yard, as he had meant to do; his departure would be, in fact, a convenience to the family. He discovered any quantity of urgent reasons for his sudden flight; for there is no such Jesuit as the desire of your heart. He hurried down at once to tell the news to his sister in L'Houmeau and to take counsel with her. As he reached Postel's shop, he bethought himself that if all other means failed, he could borrow enough to live upon for a year from his father's successor.

"Three francs per day will be abundance for me if I live with Louise," he thought; "it is only a thousand francs for a whole year. And in six months' time I shall have plenty of money."

Then, under seal and promise of secrecy, Eve and her mother heard Lucien's confidences. Both the women began to cry as they heard of the ambitious plans; and when he asked the reason of their trouble, they told him that every penny they possessed had been spent on table-linen, house-linen, Eve's wedding clothes, and on a host of things that David had overlooked. They had been so glad to do this, for David had made a marriage-settlement of ten thousand francs on Eve. Lucien then spoke of his idea of a loan, and Mme. Chardon undertook to ask M. Postel to lend them a thousand francs for a twelve-month.

"But, Lucien," said Eve, as a thought clutched at her heart, "you will not be here at my wedding! Oh! come back, I will put it off for a few days. Surely she will give you leave to come back in a fortnight, if only you go with her now? Surely, she would spare you to us for a week, Lucien, when we brought you up for her? We shall have no luck if you are not at the wedding. . . . But will a thousand francs be enough for you?" she asked, suddenly interrupting herself. "Your coat suits you divinely, but you have only that one! You have only two fine shirts, the other six are coarse linen; and three of your white ties are just common muslin, there are only two lawn cravats, and your pocket-handkerchiefs are not good ones. Where will you find a sister in Paris who will get up your linen in one day as you want it? You will want ever so much more. Then you have just the one pair of new nankeen trousers, last year's trousers are tight for you; you will be obliged to have clothes made in Paris, and Paris prices are not like Angouleme prices. You have only two presentable white waistcoats; I have mended the others already. Come, I advise you to take two thousand francs."

David came in as she spoke, and apparently heard the last two words, for he looked at the brother and sister and said nothing.

"Do not keep anything from me," he said at last.

"Well," exclaimed Eve, "he is going away with *her.*"

Mme. Chardon came in again, and, not seeing David, began at once:

"Postel is willing to lend you the thousand francs, Lucien," she said, "but only for six months; and even then he wants you to let him have a bill endorsed by your brother-in-law, for he says that you are giving him no security."

She turned and saw David, and there was a deep silence in the room. The Chardons thought how they had abused David's goodness, and felt ashamed. Tears stood in the young printer's eyes.

"Then you will not be here at our wedding," he began. "You are not going to live with us! And here have I been squandering all that I had! Oh! Lucien, as I came along, bringing Eve her little bits of wedding jewelry, I did not think that I should be sorry I spent the money on them." He brushed his hand over his eyes as he drew the little cases from his pocket.

He set down the tiny morocco-covered boxes on the table in front of his mother-in-law.

"Oh! why do you think so much for me?" protested Eve, giving him a divinely sweet smile that belied her words.

"Mamma, dear," said David, "just tell M. Postel that I will put my name to the bill, for I can tell from your face, Lucien, that you have quite made up your mind to go."

Lucien's head sank dejectedly; there was a little pause, then he said, "Do not think hardly of me, my dear, good angels."

He put his arms about Eve and David, and drew them close, and held them tightly to him as he added, "Wait and see what comes of it, and you shall know how much I love you. What is the good of our high thinking, David, if it does not enable us to disregard the petty ceremonial in which the law entangles our affections? Shall I not be with you in spirit, in spite of the distance between us? Shall we not be united in thought? Have I not a destiny to fulfil? Will publishers come here to seek my *Archer of Charles IX.* and the *Marguerites*? A little sooner or a little later I shall be obliged in any case to do as I am doing to-day, should I not? And shall I ever find a better opportunity than this? Does not my success entirely depend upon my entrance on life in Paris through the Marquise d'Espard's salon?"

"He is right," said Eve; "you yourself were saying, were you not, that he ought to go to Paris at once?"

David took Eve's hand in his, and drew her into the narrow little room where she had slept for seven years.

"Love, you were saying just now that he would want two thousand francs?" he said in her ear. "Postel is only lending one thousand."

Eve gave her betrothed a look, and he read all her anguish in her eyes.

"Listen, my adored Eve, we are making a bad start in life. Yes, my expenses have taken all my capital; I have just two thousand francs left, and half of it will be wanted to carry on the business. If we give your brother the thousand francs, it will mean that we are giving away our bread, that we shall live in anxiety. If I were alone, I know what I should do; but we are two. Decide for us."

Eve, distracted, sprang to her lover's arms, and kissed him tenderly, as she answered through her tears:

"Do as you would do if you were alone; I will work to earn the money."

In spite of the most impassioned kiss ever given and taken by betrothed lovers, David left Eve overcome with trouble, and went out to Lucien.

"Do not worry yourself," he said; "you shall have your two thousand francs."

"Go in to see Postel," said Mme. Chardon, "for you must both give your signatures to the bill."

When Lucien and David came back again unexpectedly, they found Eve and her mother on their knees in prayer. The women felt sure that Lucien's return would bring the realization of many hopes; but at the moment they could only feel how much they were losing in the parting, and the happiness to come seemed too dearly bought by an absence that broke up their life together, and would fill the coming days with innumerable fears for Lucien.

"If you could ever forget this sight," David said in Lucien's ear, "you would be the basest of men."

David, no doubt, thought that these brave words were needed; Mme. de Bargeton's influence seemed to him less to be feared than his friend's unlucky instability of character, Lucien was so easily led for good or evil. Eve soon packed Lucien's clothes; the Fernando Cortez of literature carried but little baggage. He was wearing his best overcoat, his best waistcoat, and one of the two fine shirts. The whole of his linen, the celebrated coat, and his manuscript made up so small a package that to hide it from Mme. de Bargeton, David proposed to send it by coach to a paper merchant with whom he had dealings, and wrote and advised him to that effect, and asked him to keep the parcel until Lucien sent for it.

In spite of Mme. de Bargeton's precautions, Chatelet found out that she was leaving Angouleme; and with a view to discovering whether she was traveling alone or with Lucien, he sent his man to Ruffec with instructions to watch every carriage that changed horses at that stage.

"If she is taking her poet with her," thought he, "I have her now."

Lucien set out before daybreak the next morning. David went with him. David had hired a cabriolet, pretending that he was going to Marsac on business, a little piece of deception which seemed probable under the circumstances. The two friends went to Marsac, and spent part of the day with the old "bear." As evening came on they set out again, and in the beginning of the dawn they waited in the road, on the further side of Mansle, for Mme. de Bargeton. When the seventy-year old traveling carriage, which he had many a time seen in the coach-house, appeared in sight, Lucien felt more deeply moved than he had ever been in his life before; he sprang into David's arms.

"God grant that this may be for your good!" said David, and he climbed into the shabby cabriolet and drove away with a feeling of dread clutching at his heart; he had terrible presentiments of the fate awaiting Lucien in Paris.

ADDENDUM

The following personages appear in other stories of the Human Comedy.

Bargeton, Madame de (see Chatelet, Baronne du)

Cerizet

Eve and David

A Man of Business

Scenes from a Courtesan's Life

The Middle Classes

Chardon, Madame (nee Rubempre)

Eve and David

Scenes from a Courtesan's Life

Chatelet, Sixte, Baron du

A Distinguished Provincial at Paris

Scenes from a Courtesan's Life

The Thirteen

www.ReadHowYouWant.com

You can buy our **Large Type** and **EasyRead** books from our www.ReadHowYouWant.com website, from websites like Amazon.com and through your UK and North American bookshop.

EasyRead books are designed to make your reading easy and enjoyable. **EasyRead** books are published in different font sizes, so you can select the font size best for you.

EasyRead is for people with normal eyesight who want books in an easy-to-read format.

EasyRead Comfort is for people who find reading small print tiring but do not need large print.

EasyRead Large is for people who find it easier to read larger print.

The **EasyRead** font, character, word and line spacing have all been set to make it as easy as possible both to recognize a word, and to run your eye along a line of text without losing your place. We split as few words as possible at line ends, as split words make reading harder and can be annoying. For out-of-copyright books, words have been changed to modern spelling (where the sense is not affected), and the original hyphenation of compound words has been retained where this improves word recognition or sense.

With most things you buy, you get a choice, and you can choose the make and model that suits best. There is a big exception – books. You don't get to choose a format that is easy for you to read – you have to read the format the publisher selects.

This **"One Size Fits All"** paradigm **no longer** need apply to books.

At www.ReadHowYouWant.com, you can order a book just as you want it, so you can read it easily. You can choose nearly any format, and at a surprisingly low cost, because of a technical breakthrough that allows us to typeset an individual book automatically, print and bind the book and have it quickly sent directly to you.

You can have your book in **Talking Book** formats (**DAISY or MP3**) or as an **E-book** or in **Braille**.

We have developed totally new visual formats which we hope will help people with **dyslexia** and other print reading disabilities. Look at www.ReadHowYo uWant.com for more information.

Good news for publishers and authors. There is a big market for large type, personalized and accessible format books. We can help publishers and authors find new market opportunities for their books, and selling your book through www.ReadHo wYouWant.com is easy – we do the work for you. Contact us on info@ReadHowYouWant.com.

Printed in the United Kingdom
by Lightning Source UK Ltd.
117001UKS00001B/25